"You're running scared, aren't you, Willa? Afraid of what you felt last night?"

Her cheeks heated up at the memory. "I don't sleep around."

"I didn't think you did. And I don't intend to pressure you for something you won't give freely. But I do intend to make the New Moon Ranch my home. You'd better figure out how to tolerate my presence."

The truck's engine roared to life, and Daniel gave her a grin. "'Cause come Christmas Day, I'll be a permanent fixture in your life. And it's gonna be a long fifty years if we can't even say good morning without getting in an argument!"

Then, without warning, he backed into a cloud of dust, turned sharply and headed up the road, leaving Willa behind....

Dear Reader,

My vision of the ideal Christmas includes a beautiful evergreen tree decorated with glittering ornaments, a cheerful blaze in the fireplace and lots of snow outside the windows. So I gave myself a real challenge when I decided to set a holiday book in south Texas. First of all—no snow! The weather in south Texas in December might be cool, even chilly, but it's a long way from cold enough for the white stuff. My traditional Hispanic family doesn't even put up a Christmas tree. What's a writer to do?

"Love is the reason for the season," they say. And the common theme between my ideal Christmas and Christmas at the Blue Moon Ranch is the chance to celebrate with family and friends. As the holidays arrive, Daniel Trent and Willa Mercado discover that loving each other makes this most magical time of the year even better.

I hope their story adds an extra sparkle to your own preparations for a happy holiday. *Feliz Navidad!*

All the best,

Lynnette Kent

P.S. I love to hear from readers. Feel free to drop me a note at P.O. Box 1012, Vass, NC 28394, or visit my Web site, www.lynnette-kent.com.

Christmas at
Blue Moon Ranch
Lynnette Kent

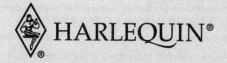

HARLEQUIN®

TORONTO • NEW YORK • LONDON
AMSTERDAM • PARIS • SYDNEY • HAMBURG
STOCKHOLM • ATHENS • TOKYO • MILAN • MADRID
PRAGUE • WARSAW • BUDAPEST • AUCKLAND

ISBN-13: 978-0-373-75191-4
ISBN-10:   0-373-75191-5

CHRISTMAS AT BLUE MOON RANCH

www.eHarlequin.com

Printed in U.S.A.

ABOUT THE AUTHOR

Lynnette Kent began writing her first romance in the fourth grade, about a ship's stowaway who would fall in love with her captain, Christopher Columbus. Years of scribbling later, her husband suggested she write one of those "Harlequin romances" she loved to read. With his patience and her two daughters' support, Lynnette realized her dream of being a published novelist. She now lives in North Carolina, where she divides her time between books—writing and reading—and the horses she adores. Feel free to contact Lynnette via her Web site, www.lynnette-kent.com, or with a letter to PMB 304, Westwood Shopping Center, Fayetteville, NC 28314.

Books by Lynnette Kent

HARLEQUIN SUPERROMANCE

765—ONE MORE RODEO
793—WHEN SPARKS FLY
824—WHAT A MAN'S GOT TO DO
868—EXPECTING THE BEST
901—LUKE'S DAUGHTERS
938—MATT'S FAMILY
988—NOW THAT YOU'RE HERE
1002—MARRIED IN MONTANA
1024—SHENANDOAH CHRISTMAS
1080—THE THIRD MRS. MITCHELL
1118—THE BALLAD OF DIXON BELL
1147—THE LAST HONEST MAN
1177—THE FAKE HUSBAND
1229—SINGLE WITH KIDS
1245—ABBY'S CHRISTMAS
1326—THE PRODIGAL TEXAN

To our military heroes and their families,
With many thanks.

Chapter One

Thunderclouds piled up on the western horizon as Willa Mercado drove into Zapata, Texas, to betray her husband.

She wasn't contemplating actual adultery. Jamie had been dead for eighteen months. She couldn't cheat on a dead man even if she wanted to. And she did not want to.

But selling the Blue Moon Ranch, which had been Mercado family land for more than a century, definitely felt like betrayal.

"Not the whole ranch," she reminded herself for the millionth time, gripping the steering wheel tightly with both hands. "You're only selling ten percent, a thousand acres. You'll never miss it. Your grandchildren will never miss it."

Even so, the guilt continued to chafe at her as she drove, like leather boots a size too small.

Her attorney, Juan Angelo, occupied an office in a strip mall near the fancy new Zapata County Courthouse. Willa whipped her truck into a parking space, pulled the key from the ignition and shoved the door open. Without giving herself a chance for more second thoughts, she grabbed up her purse and the folder of papers she needed, then strode toward the lawyer's tinted glass door. A chime sounded as she entered the air-conditioned space, and two pairs of eyes fastened on her face.

"I'm Willa Mercado," she told the pretty blonde at the reception desk. "I have an appointment for a closing at three."

"Yes, Mrs. Mercado." The young woman gave her a friendly smile. "Mr. Angelo will be free in a few minutes. Can I get you something to drink while you wait?"

Willa's hands were shaking too badly to hold a cup steady. "No, thanks."

Another bright, white smile. "Just have a seat, then. He'll be with you shortly. My name is Julie—let me know if you need anything."

Julie got up from her desk and went through a door at the back of the room. Willa turned toward the chairs arranged around the wall near the front windows and met the gaze that had been fixed on her since she'd walked in.

He sat at ease in the corner chair, one long, jean-clad leg stretched out in front of him. A soft chambray shirt and navy sports coat hung a little loosely from his wide shoulders. His bright blue eyes smiled as they met hers and he brought up a sexy, three-sided grin, which creased his cheeks and heated hers.

"Willa Mercado?" His voice made her think of warm butterscotch on cold vanilla ice cream. "I'm Daniel Trent. I think we're here on the same business."

The urge she'd felt to return that grin evaporated. Willa nodded curtly. "Major Trent." She chose a chair as far from his as possible, facing the receptionist's desk so she didn't have to confront the man who was buying part of her soul.

"Forgive me for not getting up," he said, evidently oblivious to her desire to ignore him. "My bum leg's acting up with the storm coming in."

Willa waved away the comment without looking at him. "Don't worry about it." But she couldn't stop her gaze from sliding sideways to his legs. She didn't see a cast or a brace. What did "bum leg" mean? Was it the one he kept bent, or the one he held straight? Just how disabled was he?

He still didn't take the hint. "There's a question I've been wanting to ask you ever since I first heard the name of your spread. *El Rancho Luna Azul*—the Blue Moon Ranch. Where did the name come from?"

Nosy, as well as dense. "The legend says that Rafael Mercado, who founded the ranch, spent his first night on the land under a blue moon."

Trent chuckled, a rich, deep sound. "Old Rafael must have been a romantic."

She glanced over, unable to suppress a smile. "He had his wife with him. Maybe she chose the name."

"Women being more imaginative? Maybe." He lifted a quizzical eyebrow. "Does that mean Rafael was henpecked?"

Before she could answer, Julie reappeared. "Mrs. Mercado? Major Trent? Right this way. Mr. Angelo's got everything ready."

Willa took a deep breath and stood up, then glanced Daniel Trent in time to see him pick up a cane from the floor. She couldn't look away as he propped the stick in front of him, then held it with both hands for extra support as he came up out of the chair, using only the strength of the bent left leg. His right leg stayed straight. When he stepped forward, he swung that stiff leg out to the side in a rolling sort of gait.

Daniel Trent caught her staring, of course, and shrugged one shoulder. "Like I said, the weather." Leaning one-handed on the cane, he motioned her ahead of him with the other. "Shall we?"

Without the mesmerizing smile to distract her, she could see the stress in his face, the lines at the corners of his eyes and around his mouth, which revealed a pain he didn't want to acknowledge.

A twinge of sympathy lodged in Willa's chest. "Sure." She followed Julie down the hall. About halfway along, though, her second thoughts hit like a rampaging longhorn bull. She actually stumbled in shock.

A warm hand closed around her elbow from behind. "Are you okay?"

Her cheeks hot with embarrassment, she glanced back at Daniel Trent. "I'm fine. Sorry."

He let go easily as she pulled free. "No problem."

Frowning, Willa hurried to catch up with the secretary. Maybe she was making a huge mistake. When she'd put the land up for sale, she'd expected to get a man with experience, a steady and reliable neighbor she could depend on. What kind of ranching background did Daniel Trent have? How would he manage cattle if he couldn't walk without a limp? Did he have other plans for the land that she should know about?

At the end of the hallway, attorney Juan Angelo waited for them in a windowless conference room. "Willa, good to see you again. I've got your papers right here." He pulled out a chair at one corner of the long table that filled most of the available space and scooted it in underneath her. Then he went to shake hands with Daniel Trent.

"I'm glad to meet you, Major Trent. I've arranged your paperwork, too." He glanced at the cane, and rolled back a chair on the other corner. "Have a seat."

Willa understood, from the way Daniel pressed his lips together, how much he disliked that accommodation to his disability. But he said, "Thanks," and lowered himself into the chair without much trouble. Now they sat facing each other, with the attorney at the head of the table between them.

Juan rubbed his hands together. "So, we're here to close on the sale of a thousand acres of ranch land. Willa, you're the seller, of course, and Daniel is the buyer. We've got a fair amount of paperwork to go through, but nothing too complicated. This first page—"

Willa put up a hand. "Just a minute." Her reservations had seized control, and now she looked Daniel Trent straight in the eye. "I know I should have asked this before, but better late than never. Just what are you planning to do with this land, if you buy it?"

Daniel Trent didn't avoid her gaze. The lift of his eyebrow remarked on her use of *if.*

The attorney cleared his throat. "Willa, you shouldn't—"

She glanced at Juan. "I think I have a right to know if he's got something planned that's going to affect my operation, my business. Like a trailer park or a factory or an oil refinery."

"But—"

"It's okay," Daniel said. "I don't mind answering the question." The smile had returned to his eyes. "I'm planning to use the land just as you have. I want to raise cattle and a few horses. I'm planning to be a rancher." That devastating grin came into play. "I thought I'd call it New Moon Ranch."

Willa didn't smile back. "Do you have a ranching background?"

He shook his head. "Not much. I've spent the past twelve years in the Army."

"Do you have any experience with cattle? Horses?" Could he handle the rustlers who'd been preying on her herd?

"Growing up in Ohio, I had a pony. As a teenager, I spent summers working on a dude ranch in Wyoming. But I haven't done any riding recently. The U.S. cavalry," he said with a smile, "got phased out a while back."

So she wouldn't be able to depend on his help in stopping the cattle thieves preying on her herd. Willa dropped back against her chair. "How do you expect to be able to run a ranch? With just a few months of experience and…and—"

"And a bum leg," he finished for her.

"Well, yes. How in the world are you going to make this work?"

"I think Major Trent's plans are his own business, Willa." Juan's plump face had turned a deep red and his eyes had gotten very wide, with all the whites showing. "We're just here to complete the sale."

"I figured I could hire good hands to help me out," Daniel explained. "And I'm not too proud to ask my neighbors for advice, maybe a little assistance now and then."

"Ranching is a full-time job." Boy, did she know that. "Running a ranch, even a small one, requires stamina and strength, coordination and physical competence." Which was why she was always exhausted at the end of each and every day. "The economics are against you, too. Running such a small herd—one, two hundred head—you'll barely break even most years. The price of corn is going up and water's been scarce. Do you know how to handle those problems? Why do you want to take on a complicated enterprise that's pretty much guaranteed to fail?"

"Willa…" Juan groaned.

Daniel Trent straightened up in his chair, and suddenly she could see the military training behind his easy-going facade. "I may not be a hundred percent physically, but I expect to make a profit on the New Moon."

"I'm sure you will," Juan started. "And I'm sure—"

"I'm not." Willa flattened her hands on the table. "And I don't think I can complete the sale under these conditions."

The attorney choked. Trent narrowed his eyes. "You're backing out on the deal?"

"This land is my children's heritage. I have a duty to see that it's cared for properly."

"I can do that."

"How do I know? How do you know?"

Juan got to his feet. "Willa, can I talk to you privately for a moment? Excuse us, Daniel." He walked to the door and opened it, waited for Willa to go through and then followed her out into the narrow hallway. With the door shut again, he faced her, his hands propped on his hips.

"What in the world do you think you're doing?"

Willa winced as she heard the attorney's urgent question.

He rushed on before she could answer. "You're throwing away this sale is what you're doing. Why?"

"I can't sell the land, Juan. Especially not to someone who knows next to nothing about ranching, or cattle." She rubbed her eyes with her fingers. "I might as well poison the water and set fire to the grass."

"Do I have to remind you of how much you'll be making off this sale? Daniel Trent didn't argue with the price, didn't try to talk you down. He paid top dollar and all he wants to do is run a few head of beef and some horses. It's not that big a deal."

"That land is the Mercado legacy. I want to know it's taken care of." *I wanted some help!* She bit her lip to keep the words unsaid.

"So let me remind you about the taxes you owe on that land. About the outstanding bills at the feed store and the veterinarian, the payroll you're behind on. Remember the mortgage Jamie took out on the ranch, and the fact that you have kids who'll be wanting to go to college in just a few years. You need this cash, Willa. As your attorney, I'm recommending you march in there, keep your mouth shut and sign those papers."

She stared at him in the dim light of the hall, hating the truth, unable to decide. They both jumped when the door to the conference room opened.

Daniel Trent stood silhouetted by the fluorescent light behind him, his shoulders slanted slightly, his hip cocked to the side by that stiff leg. "If you two want to come back, I think I have a solution to this dilemma."

BY THE TIME THEY'D FINISHED, Daniel's leg felt like a fallen tree with a host of termites chewing on it from the inside out. The extra paperwork he'd suggested had extended the meeting by almost an hour, which meant he was two hours past the time for his usual dose of pain meds. He only took over-the-counter stuff these days, but the drugs still made a difference.

As a distraction, he let himself gaze at Willa Mercado while she finished reading the agreement he'd proposed. She might have a heart of stone, but he found her incredibly sexy—her thick black hair, tamed into a shiny braid hanging down her back, her smooth olive skin, her wide, long-lashed dark eyes. Thin and graceful, she reminded him of a gazelle, all legs and arms, with the potential for great speed and endurance. Her mouth fascinated him, and he couldn't seem to look away from the sensual promise of those wide, full lips.

A promise likely to remain unfilled, he told himself. She'd agreed to let him live on the portion of the Blue Moon he'd wanted to buy, but she wasn't happy about it. At his suggestion, she'd put him on probation. After three months, if she didn't think he'd demonstrated an aptitude for ranching life, the sale contract would be void and he'd be out on his ear while she kept his deposit as rent.

Willa finished reading and, without a word, picked up a nearby pen to sign the last sheet. She passed the page to Juan, who gave it to Daniel for his signature. After three copies had been completed, the lawyer rubbed his hands together in satisfaction.

"That's great. I think this is an excellent solution." Stacking the papers together, he practically beamed. "Daniel, you'll have a chance to make sure this is what you want, and Willa, you'll be able to see that you're doing the right thing in selling Daniel this parcel of land. I'll have Julie make an appointment for three months from now, and we'll all get back together to finalize the sale."

He bustled out, leaving the door open, but returned before Daniel had a chance to say anything to the woman across the table.

"I just looked at the calendar," Juan said. "Three months from today will be Christmas Eve. I thought I'd ask whether you want to set something up after the New Year." He gave an apologetic shrug. "Our office is usually closed that last week of December."

Willa opened her mouth, but Daniel spoke first. "Set it up for December twenty-first," he said. "I plan to spend Christmas on the New Moon Ranch."

He heard the click of teeth as Willa snapped her jaws shut.

WITH THEIR BUSINESS COMPLETED—for good or for ill, and Willa wasn't sure which—Juan led them back to the front of the office, where the sound of rain drumming on the roof resembled the thunder of stampeding cattle. The storm had arrived with a vengeance.

"I've been listening to the weather," Julie volunteered. "They're predicting flash floods for the rest of today and tonight, plus the possibility of tornadoes."

"A bad night to travel." Juan stood between Willa and Daniel as they stared out at the downpour. "Willa, you should probably stay in town for the evening, go home tomorrow after the storm passes. La Casa Motel, just down the road, is a pretty nice place."

"I've got a spare umbrella." Julie came to stand beside her. "You're welcome to use it to get to your car."

"Thanks." Willa held the door open with her shoulder and opened the umbrella just outside. As she started out into the deluge, Daniel Trent took her place in the doorway. Still sheltered by the roof over the walk, Willa obeyed the prompting of her better nature and waved at him to join her. "Come on—we can share."

His sunny smile seemed to brighten the weather. "I don't mind if I do. I'm no fan of drowning." He joined her under the umbrella, automatically reaching for the curved handle.

But her hand was already there, and for a moment his warm, dry palm closed over her fingers. Willa gave a little gasp as the friction between his skin and hers set off tingles that ran up her arm and into her chest. Standing so close to her, Daniel Trent was much bigger than she'd realized, his frame more imposing. She felt sheltered, having him between her and the storm.

"Your truck's closer," he said, bending his head to speak into her ear, and another shiver swept through her. "Let's go that way."

Willa nodded. Three inches of water had pooled on the asphalt parking lot, soaking into her one pair of good dress shoes with each step. Alone, she would have sprinted through the rain to the truck but, thinking of Daniel's leg, she matched her speed to the one he set. By the time they reached her truck, her slacks were soaked from the knees down.

"Thank God for remote keys," she said, pulling the door open as soon as she could touch the handle. Daniel raised the umbrella to shelter her while she climbed in, then backed away as soon as she got seated. With the cane in one hand and the umbrella in the other, he gave her a nod before turning toward a shiny silver pickup parked several rows over from hers. He'd bought himself a fancy new truck to go with his new ranch.

Willa squeezed her eyes shut. She intended to deny him his ranch…his dream. Guilt pounded in her temples and throbbed at the back of her neck.

Or maybe that was hunger. Breakfast had happened before sunrise and she'd skipped lunch to finish up her chores prior to heading into town. Even if she didn't stay the night, she could check into La Casa Motel for a few hours, get a nap and a good meal before the drive home. She'd have to deal with Daniel Trent as a neighbor soon enough. Then she'd know whether she should feel guilty at the bargain she'd struck…or relieved.

DANIEL HAD STAYED AT LA CASA the night before, so he bypassed the reception area for the side door closest to the elevator. He'd bolted down some pain pills with the dregs of a soda he'd left in the truck. Now he just needed to stretch out on a bed and wait for them to take effect.

His stomach woke him up an hour later, growling like a grizzly bear at the end of winter. As he stripped off his damp shirt and jeans to take a shower, he kept his back to the mirror. All his life, he'd taken his functional, unscarred body for granted, and he still wasn't adjusted to the new reality. The last woman he'd dated hadn't even wanted to try.

In the motel dining room, he chose a table giving him a view of the thunderstorm still raging outside and savored the tart flavor of a margarita as he watched rain sheeting the windows. Willa Mercado just might be stubborn enough to believe she could drive through this kind of weather, but Daniel hoped she was smarter than that. He was tempted to try to reach her through the hotel switchboard, just to see if she'd checked in. Otherwise, he'd probably spend the night worrying about her.

Even as the thought occurred to him, she appeared at the entrance to the restaurant. She looked more relaxed than she had at the lawyer's office, and the smile she gave the hostess was downright friendly. Daniel thought he'd have to try to earn himself a few of Willa Mercado's smiles.

Thanks to the pain medicine, he got to his feet fairly smoothly as she approached his table. "Good evening," he said, as she jerked to a stop upon seeing him. "I'd be happy to have you join me."

The hostess assumed Willa would agree and disappeared. From the line between Willa's arched eyebrows, though, Daniel wasn't so sure. "Please?" he said.

She took in a deep breath and then blew it out. "Sure. Thanks." Once seated, she folded her arms on the table and stared straight at him. "You look better."

Her perception startled him. "I…um…got a nap. And some pills."

"For the bum leg." The corner of her mouth quirked—nearly a smile.

"Right."

"Were you in a car accident?"

He shrugged. "You could say that. My truck ran over an IED in Iraq. That's an—"

She held up a hand. "I know what it is. Improvised explosive device. My husband Jamie was killed by one. In Iraq."

Daniel swore under his breath. "I'm sorry." Grabbing his cane, he started to get up. "The last thing I want to do is remind you of your loss. I'll let you enjoy your dinner in peace."

Willa could have let him go. She'd looked forward to dinner by herself, hadn't wanted to share a meal with this…this intruder.

Yet she found herself on her feet, putting a hand on his arm to stop him before he moved away.

"Don't leave, Daniel." She met his troubled blue gaze with an apologetic smile. "I'm sorry I've been so rude. We can't go anywhere else while this storm lasts, and we're going to be neighbors. Let's get to know each other."

Chapter Two

By the time their salads were served, Willa was no longer surprised to find herself chuckling, even laughing aloud, at some of Daniel's comments. He possessed a wealth of stories about his travels with the Army, along with a charming, humorous way of telling them.

She'd offered a few details about her family—thirteen-year-old twins Robbie and Susannah, ten-year-old Toby, plus Jamie's aunts, Rosa and Lilianna, who lived with them and took care of the house. The margarita she'd enjoyed with their tortilla chips and salsa had helped her relax, of course. Now they were sharing a pitcher of sangria, a temptation she hadn't indulged in since before Jamie had left. For the first time in more than two years, Willa allowed her worries to slip to the back of her mind while she concentrated on the here and now.

"Here and now" being an incredibly attractive man who seemed to be enjoying himself very much indeed. She took a sip of the wine, then another, and voiced the question that had been on her mind all afternoon. "What made you decide to take up ranching? I mean...you don't have the background, or a family connection. And it's not exactly a career the military trains you for, right?"

"Right." He watched the wine slosh gently as he rolled the

stem of his goblet between two fingers. "I guess it sounds pretty crazy. Everybody I've talked to thinks so…including you." His grin flashed. "It was about a year ago, I guess, I was sitting in some doctor's office for what seemed like appointment one thousand, facing more surgery and time in a hospital bed. I picked up one of those magazines about the West, and started looking at an article on some big actor's 'alternative lifestyle.'"

With a glance at her face, he continued. "Gorgeous scenery, working outside in the fresh air and sunshine with animals and nature—what's not to like?"

Willa rolled her eyes. "I could give you a list a mile long."

He held up a hand. "Leave me my illusions, for a few more days, at least. After twelve years in the Army, I knew I wanted to be my own boss, make my own decisions. Ranching seemed to me—still seems—like an independent, productive way to live."

Willa decided to forbear commenting on his naiveté. "I haven't seen too many famous actors buying up land in Zapata County. So why did you decide on south Texas? What made you decide to buy my…this particular piece of land? How many other ranches did you see?"

Daniel shook his head. "Not a single one. I read your ad…'For Sale, 1000 Acres of the beautiful Wild Horse Desert in the heart of Texas cattle country. House and barn ready for occupation. Your dream is waiting!'" He pretended to slap himself, first one cheek and then the other. "That's all it took."

Willa gazed at him in confusion. "When did you come down to visit? Seems like I would have met…" She stumbled to a stop as he shook his head.

"I didn't visit. I liked the sound of the Wild Horse Desert and Texas. There was a house and a barn and a thousand acres of land. I didn't need to know anything else. I called the real estate agent that afternoon and made the offer."

The idea of such impetuosity left Willa breathless and uneasy. "That's…that's a big risk, don't you think? With a lot of money?"

He shrugged one shoulder. "My parents left me a healthy life insurance policy and some very smart investments. Sometimes you have to go with your gut instincts. And my instincts tell me that the New Moon ranch is just what I want." He leaned toward her, holding out the pitcher. "More wine?"

"I shouldn't." But she didn't draw her glass away. Yes, she was a little buzzed, but what was the harm? The kids were safe at home—she'd called to check on them and the ranch before she'd come down to dinner. And she wouldn't be driving tonight, thanks to the storm. After two years of being in charge, of always staying in control, couldn't she have just one carefree evening?

"Such a serious face," Daniel said. "What are you thinking about?"

Willa shook her head, then blew out a deep breath of relief. "Responsibility, and how good it feels to let go a little."

Daniel nodded, and held up his own wineglass in a toast. "To freedom," he said.

Smiling, Willa clinked her rim against his. "To freedom." They drank, holding each other's gazes, and she felt a quiver deep inside, where nothing had stirred for a long, long time.

"Fajitas?" a distant voice said. "Enchiladas royale?"

"Dinner." Willa broke her connection with Daniel and looked at the waiter. "Just in time. I'm…um…starving."

"Me, too," she heard Daniel murmur. "Me, too."

SEVERAL HOURS LATER, WILLA leaned a shoulder against the wall as she and Daniel waited for the elevator. "I haven't had this much to drink in years," she confessed. "I'll be sorry tomorrow morning."

"Me, too." He nodded slowly. "But sometimes you just have to cut loose, you know?"

The door beside her slid open and Willa tipped herself inside the elevator. "I guess. And you do tell some outrageously hila…hilarious jokes."

With a line of concentration between his eyebrows, Daniel studied the elevator control panel. "What floor are you on?"

"Three."

His eyebrows lifted in surprise. "Me, too." After a couple of misses, he managed to stab the button. "Funny we didn't see each other earlier."

"Funny." The car started with a jerk and the spin in Willa's head accelerated. She balanced against the wall behind her and closed her eyes, which did not help, so she opened them to look straight across at Daniel. He was smiling as he looked back at her. Through the haze of alcohol surrounding them, she recognized the glint in his eyes for what it was. Desire, pure and simple. Daniel Trent was thinking about taking her to bed.

She'd been thinking the same thing about him for the past hour…or four drinks, whichever lasted longer.

Fortunately, the elevator door slid open and saved her from literally jumping his bones. Willa stepped carefully across the metal threshold and studied the sign on the opposite wall.

"My room's this way." She swayed to the left. "G'night."

"Mine is, too." Daniel followed her. She could feel him behind her, big and warm and sexy. *Damn him.*

Concentrating hard, Willa read the room numbers as she walked along. "This is me. 334." She slid the key card in, took it out and turned it around so the arrow pointed in the right direction, then tried again. "'Night."

"334." Daniel nodded. "I'm 343." As she looked back, he braced a hand on the wall beside her head and stood for a second just gazing at her. Reading his face, she knew all she'd have to do was ask him in. He'd take over from there. He wanted her. She wanted him. Badly.

"Good night," Willa said distinctly, emphatically. Then she tripped into the hallway of her room, turned and shut the door in his handsome face.

"'Night, Willa," he said from the other side. With her cheek pressed against the door panel, she heard him whistling as he moved further down the hall, toward 343. The whistling stopped, and she could visualize Daniel focusing on getting the key card into the slot correctly.

"Damn." He said the word softly, but with feeling. In another second, he swore again…and again, with more force.

Willa opened her door and peered down the hall. Daniel stood at the very end, next to the emergency exit, jabbing his key card into the lock.

He glanced back her way. "It won't open." Growling low in his throat, he raised a fist to pound on the door. "Dammit, the damn key won't work."

As he drew back his arm for another round of pounding, the door panel flew open. A short, round-bellied, gray-haired man stood on the threshold in a T-shirt and red plaid boxer shorts. "What the hell do you think you're doing?"

Daniel barely managed to avoid punching the guy in the face. The effort sent him staggering backward, up against the opposite wall. "This is my room!"

"This damn sure isn't your room. And if you don't shut up and get out I'm going to call security and the cops!" The door slammed shut.

Daniel closed his eyes and dropped his spinning head back against the wall. "Why is he in my room? Where am I gonna sleep?" He hadn't been drunk in a long, long time. He hadn't been this frustrated in even longer.

Cool fingers closed around his wrist. "Come on," Willa said as he opened his eyes. "You can call the front desk from my room and find out what's going on."

Her touch soothed him like a soft salve on a hot burn. Blowing out a deep breath, Daniel followed without argument. Inside her dimly lit room, he dropped to sit on one of the beds and punched O on the phone. "This is Daniel Trent. I'm trying to get into my room—my key won't work and there's a guy already in there. What's going on?"

A bored voice asked, "What room number is that, Mr. Trent?"

"My room. 343. Why is there someone else in my room?"

After a pause, the voice said, "Um…that's not your room, Mr. Trent. You've mistaken the number."

Daniel swore. "Well, what's the right number?"

Another hesitation. "I can't tell you that over the phone, Mr. Trent. If you'll come down to the front desk and produce some I.D., we'll be happy to give you the room number."

"Oh, for God's sake. It's just a room. Tell me the number and let me go to bed!"

"I can't do that without being certain of who you are. Our guests' security—"

Daniel grunted and hung up the phone. "Great. I have to go back downstairs and give them some I.D. before they'll tell me what room I'm in."

Willa sat on the other bed, facing him, frankly laughing. "You've forgotten your room number?"

He rolled his eyes. "I haven't had that much alcohol in quite a while." Propping his cane in front of him, he pulled himself to his feet. "I'll get out of your—"

The stick tilted. His head swirled, his balance deserted him and suddenly he was falling forward. Toward Willa. Daniel managed to twist enough to avoid landing on her, but his weak leg wouldn't support his weight. He bounced onto the mattress beside her.

Laughing hard, Willa fell back to lie beside him.

"I didn't do that on purpose," Daniel said. "I told you—"

"I know. We've both had too much to drink." She wiped her eyes, still laughing. "What a disaster."

"Yeah." He propped himself on an elbow and looked down at her. "You're beautiful when you laugh."

She sniffed and wiped her eyes again. "That's quite a line."

"No line." He touched her cheek with his fingertips. "Soft. Smooth."

"Daniel…"

"You can stop me," he told her as he leaned closer. "Just say no." A slight press of his fingers turned her face toward his. He brushed his lips across hers. "Just say no."

He made another pass across that wide, generous mouth, but he didn't hear a word. Her hand came up and cupped the back of his neck, bringing him even closer. And then he was kissing Willa Mercado for all he was worth.

Willa couldn't believe how good it felt. How good *he* felt. The size and weight of him, the warmth of him surrounding her, seemed like a miracle. She'd been so cold for so long.

His mouth skimmed hers, lingered, plundered. He tasted of tequila and lime, but also something essentially, basically male. He smelled like soap and clean clothes and good man. As he kissed his way across her cheek and down her throat, she buried her face in the bend of his neck and breathed deeply of that wonderful scent.

Like magic, the buttons of her blouse came undone. For a second the air chilled her bare skin, but then Daniel chased the cold away, pressing kisses on her breast bone, the balls of her shoulders, the hollow between her breasts and everywhere in between. Willa sighed, and in the next moment her bra disappeared. First his hand claimed her and then his mouth, and she cried out at the shock of pleasure.

She went a little crazy after that, desperate for more of…well, everything. Her fingers fumbled with the buttons of his shirt, and she gave up after the second one to pull the damn thing over his head. To her surprise, he wore a plain white T-shirt underneath, yet another barrier. When she reached for the hem, though, Daniel drew back.

"Don't," he said raggedly, and bent to kiss the inner curve of her elbow. "I'm not nearly as gorgeous as you are."

Willa gasped at the stroke of his tongue against her skin, and forgot to argue with him. A few minutes later he eased her slacks over her hips. Once he'd dragged his palm along the length of her legs, she wasn't sure she remembered her own name.

"Daniel," she whispered, arching closer, wrapping a leg around his hips to draw him nearer still. Hard met soft, and she moaned. "Please. Please, tell me we don't have to stop."

She heard his low chuckle, saw a flash of that fabulous grin. He backed off enough to unfasten and strip off his jeans.

"Not a chance. I was a Boy Scout." He jerked his wallet out of the discarded pants and pulled out a duo of condoms. In the second he used to break open one package, Willa stroked her hand up his thigh, underneath the hem of his pale blue boxers.

Instead of the smooth skin and firm muscle she expected, the flesh she touched was a landscape of ridges and valleys, hard and harsh.

Daniel froze, and she looked at him in horror. "My God," Willa said. "Those are…scars?"

He nodded, then took a deep breath. "Sorry." With an awkward shift of his hips, he started to move away.

But Willa came with him. "No. Daniel, don't." On her knees behind him, she put her arms around his shoulders and her head on his shoulder. "Don't."

His shoulders lifted on a deep breath. "I wasn't thinking. I know what I look like. I shouldn't have subjected—"

"Hush." She sat back on her heels and grasped the hem of the

T-shirt. He jerked, clearly wanting to escape, but she put a hand on his shoulder. "Stay." Biting her lower lip, she deliberately peeled up the white T-shirt, uncovering the mutilated skin of his back. Tears rolled down her face as Willa studied the map of purple grooves and red hills she'd revealed.

"I'm so sorry." She put a finger gently on one of the scars. "So sorry." The pain he'd endured was unimaginable. How had he even survived? If Jamie had come back to her like this...how would he have felt? What would she have done?

"It's okay." Daniel pulled down the T-shirt again and shifted to face her. "I'm okay. Really. Don't cry, Willa." He wiped her cheeks with his thumbs, then bent to give her a quick kiss.

She understood he meant to leave without finishing what they'd started. But despite seeing the horrors he'd suffered, Willa didn't want to let him go. Even as he drew back, she circled her arms around his neck.

"Stay."

His eyebrows drew together, his blue eyes questioning, doubtful. "Are you sure?"

"Oh, yes."

He squeezed his eyes shut for a second. "Thank God."

And then he came back to her, stronger, more demanding than before. The room heated up, or maybe that was just her body, on fire everywhere Daniel touched her, everywhere he kissed. And that was *everywhere.* Finally, they lay together, skin to skin. He moved inside of her...gently, at first, then harder, faster, till the bed rocked and her body thrashed and her senses exploded into a brilliant climax. Before she could catch a single breath, Daniel gave a strangled cry.

And then he relaxed, falling to the side, drawing her with him into the shelter of the covers and his arms. Safe and sated, Willa plunged mindlessly into sleep.

SHE WOKE UP WINCING, WITH A headache thudding like a bass drum between her ears. Through one squinted eye she saw the yellow line of sunlight at the top of the drapes, which meant she must have slept much later than she'd intended.

In the next second, Willa realized she was naked under the covers. Then she remembered why.

With a gasp, she whipped her head around to see that the other side of the bed was empty. She had a moment to sigh in relief before her stomach revolted and sent her running for the bathroom.

After a few unpleasant minutes, she wiped her face with a cold washcloth. Unable to meet her own eyes in the mirror, she sat on the end of the bed she…they…hadn't slept in, her fists clenched in her lap, and faced the shameful facts.

Last night, she'd abandoned the last ounce of good sense she possessed to have sex with a man she didn't know, a man who hadn't even stayed long enough to say "Good morning." After fourteen years of marriage and three kids, she should know better than to take this kind of risk.

Every woman had the right to be stupid once in her life, especially as a teenager. Giving in to a boy's persuasion—"If you loved me you'd do it"—was understandable when you were only sixteen.

But what excuse did she have at thirty-two? How could she have allowed her principles to be overturned by a sexy grin and a pair of sweet blue eyes?

Well, no more. As she jerked on her clothes, Willa swore to herself that she wouldn't let Daniel Trent get to her. She would keep her distance, make him keep his. With any luck, he'd fail miserably in his attempt at ranching and be gone well before Christmas. All she had to do was wait him out…

…and never again give herself a chance to make a mistake like the one last night.

WHEN SHE FINALLY DREDGED UP the courage to leave her room, she found Daniel Trent leaning against the wall in the hotel lobby, scanning a newspaper.

"Good morning." Smiling, he straightened and fell into step beside her. "Can you join me for breakfast?"

"No. Thanks." She glanced at the people moving around them as if looking for someone, avoiding his knowing blue eyes. "I need to get on the road. I can't afford to miss a whole day's work."

"Okay." He folded the paper under his arm. "I thought I'd follow you out to the ranch, look around a bit. My stuff won't be arriving until the end of the week, but I'd like to see the setup, get a feel for what kind of supplies I'll be needing." Out of the corner of her eye, she saw him shrug. "I've lived in army housing most of the time, so I don't have much furniture. Outfitting a house is a new experience."

Panic erupted in her chest. Without answering, Willa walked quickly outside, aware that Daniel was following as fast as he could. She didn't slow down for him.

Somehow, though, he was right behind her when she opened her truck door. He put a hand on her arm as she started to climb in.

"Willa? What's going on?"

She threw her purse into the passenger seat and jerked around to face him. "What's going on is that I've made two horrible mistakes in the past twenty-four hours. I'm furious with myself and—"

"With me," he said, interrupting.

"Yes." She shook off his touch. "I should never have put that land up for sale, and I shouldn't have let you talk me into this crazy arrangement we've got set up now. All that was bad enough." Taking a deep breath, she tried to steady her voice. "But to know that I let myself get drunk enough to…to—" The words stayed stuck in her throat. How could she have been so careless, so disrespectful of herself?

Daniel didn't have the same scruples. "Sleep with me?"

Willa clenched her hands into fists. "Stop that! I don't want you reading my mind and finishing my thoughts."

Daniel raised his hand and stepped backward, out of her reach. "Yes, ma'am." His gaze had gone cold, and his mouth was a hard, straight line. "I will be following you as you drive home, however, because I have a contract that allows me access to the thousand acres of land I'm calling the New Moon Ranch. You should expect to see me from time to time, since the road to my place goes by the main house of the Blue Moon. I'll try not to inconvenience you as I get settled."

He pivoted on his good leg and moved away with that awkward limp, climbed into his rain-spattered truck and let the engine idle, waiting for Willa to lead the way.

Swearing under her breath, she started her own vehicle and left the parking lot. All through the hour-long drive home, she was aware of him behind her, his face grim through the windshield. He wore mirrored sunglasses, but she could imagine the blue gaze behind them. She'd read the hurt there before anger had replaced it.

Last night, she'd urged him to stay and make love with her, accepting him despite his terrible scars. This morning, she'd rejected every moment they'd spent together. That made *three* terrible mistakes she had committed in the past twenty-four hours. Willa couldn't believe how badly she'd behaved. No doubt about it, Daniel Trent brought out the worst in her. Yet another reason to avoid him.

With every mile that passed, the screw of nerves inside her twisted tighter. By the time she reached the familiar gateway— an iron arch spelling out *El Rancho Luna Azul,* with a crescent moon on each end—Willa was a wreck. Abruptly, she steered her truck to the side of the road just inside the entrance and cut the engine. Daniel stopped behind her, but she reached his window before he could open his door, so he rolled down the glass.

"Something else wrong?" he asked in a cold voice.

"Stay away from me," she told him. "If you need help, I'll send one of my workmen to do what he can. But leave me alone."

Daniel took off his sunglasses, and she was surprised to see the laughter in his eyes. "You're running scared, aren't you, Willa? Afraid of what you felt last night?"

Her cheeks heated up at the memory. "I don't sleep around."

"I didn't think you did. And I don't intend to pressure you for something you won't give freely." He slipped the shades back onto his face. "But I do intend to make the New Moon Ranch my home. You'd better figure out how to tolerate my presence."

The truck engine roared, and Daniel gave her a grin. "'Cause come Christmas Day, I'll be a permanent fixture in your life. And it's gonna be a long fifty years if we can't even say good morning without getting into an argument!"

Then, without warning, he backed into a cloud of dust, turned sharply and headed up the road, leaving Willa behind.

Chapter Three

A mile inside the Blue Moon gate, Daniel came over a rise and saw the Mercado ranch house sitting off to his right. Easing off the gas and unclenching his jaw, he slowed down for a good look at Willa's home.

He'd gleaned a little of the ranch history from the attorney and the Internet, enough to know that Rafael Mercado from Mexico had taken possession of the land in the 1840s, back when Indian attacks were an ever-present threat. The tall, defensive wall Rafael had first built around the house had been lowered in the twentieth century to reveal the courtyard, filled with mature live oak trees, which surrounded the villa inside. A series of white-columned arches created a wide veranda along the two-story front wing of the house. Two side wings stretched back at right angles to form a U-shape with another courtyard in the center. Green shutters framed the windows, a sharp contrast to the creamy white stucco walls.

Daniel squeezed a whistle through his teeth. Willa had a right to be protective—this was quite a showplace. He could imagine how much maintenance work would be involved in caring for such a property. Around the house stretched ten thousand acres of the Wild Horse Desert, where she bred and raised longhorn cattle. No doubt about it, the woman carried a heavy burden. And since her husband had died, she'd carried it alone.

At the sound of her truck rumbling up behind him, he squeezed the accelerator and pulled away fast enough to spray gravel as he fishtailed on his way. The last thing he needed was another "get lost" lecture. She'd made her point and it was a sharp one, especially after last night's pleasure.

Following the winding, hilly road farther into the Blue Moon, he saw the barns, corrals and utility buildings that formed the heart of the ranching operation. Miles of wire fencing defined the pastures, which alternated between cultivated range land and the scrubby shrubs and natural grasses native to south Texas. The wild landscape held a beauty all its own, however, especially on the morning after rainstorms had cleared the dust from the air. Daniel appreciated the wide blue Texas sky, the varied shapes of the trees and cacti and bushes, the freshness of the wind.

There was no sign to tell him when he crossed onto his own property, just a line on the map the attorney had provided. The terrain didn't change. There were fences, and cattle…although he was sure Willa would have those rounded up and removed soon enough. She wouldn't want to leave any of her property under his control.

As he came over the top of yet another hill, he realized he'd reached his destination—the foreman's cottage he'd be living in. Sited on a bare stretch of ground with only a few prickly shrubs to soften the sandy dirt, the house lacked any evidence of architectural imagination. An uncovered stoop anchored the cement-block structure, its plain front door painted a dull gray like the rest of the building. Daniel pulled into the shade of the carport attached to the side of the house and sighed as he switched off the engine. For the first time since beginning this crazy venture, he felt a little daunted.

Inside, the rooms were clean, bare and equally uninspiring. Willa hadn't gone to any lengths to make him feel welcome.

Outside once again, he drove toward the barn associated with his property, visible about a quarter of a mile away from the house. The weathered, metal-sided building, surrounded by dry, dusty corrals, did little to bolster his confidence that he could develop a functional ranching business in this place. He was stuck out here in the desert with scant practical knowledge, few ranching skills and no support.

Maybe Willa would win, after all.

Within the barn, years—decades, maybe—of discarded equipment loomed in the corners and cluttered the aisle between stalls, which appeared to have not been cleaned for about the same amount of time. What would he do with all this space once he got it cleared out? His first task, he guessed, would be to hire a foreman. Somebody with in-depth experience, somebody who knew what the hell was supposed to happen next.

What actually happened next was that somewhere, in a far corner of the cavernous building, someone sneezed.

"Hello?" Daniel welcomed the prospect of a trespasser to take his mind off the mess he'd gotten himself into. "Who's there?"

When no one answered, he walked down the aisle, peering into the stalls as he went. "Come on...I heard you. Do I have to say gesundheit before you make an appearance? Consider it said."

He stopped by a narrow wooden ladder leading to the loft above the main floor and waited, without result. Then, a minute later, came another sneeze. And another. And yet a fourth.

"Bless you." Daniel leaned his shoulder against a stall door to take the weight off his aching leg. "I'm not leaving, so you can stay hidden and sneeze your brains out or join me in the fresh air."

A revealing scuffle came from overhead. He looked up and found a face looking down at him over the edge of the loft.

"You can't really sneeze your brains out." Under a pint-sized Resistol cowboy hat, the boy was about ten, with dark eyes, nut-brown skin and shiny black hair.

"Are you sure?" Daniel couldn't mistake the kid's resemblance to Willa. This must be the youngest boy. *Toby, right?*

"Yeah. It just feels that way." The face disappeared, to be replaced by a pair of boots reaching for the top rung of the ladder. In the next second, the kid landed with a thud on the barn floor. He turned around to confront Daniel, his hands propped on his hips and his eyebrows drawn together. In his hat, his well-worn blue-checked shirt and his weathered jeans, he looked like a miniature cowpoke. "You must be the new guy."

"I must be. My name's Daniel Trent."

The boy gave a single nod, like an aristocrat acknowledging a peasant. "I'm Toby Mercado. This is my ranch."

Daniel decided not to dispute the issue at that moment. "It's a nice place, from what I've seen so far." He looked around them and shrugged. "Although this doesn't look exactly encouraging."

Toby nodded. "We haven't used this barn for a long time, not since our foreman got his own land and decided to live there. You'll have to bring in your own equipment."

"What kind of equipment?"

The dark eyes went round. "Man, you need tractors and seeders and spreaders and rakes and chains and trailers. You need tools for building and mending fences, just for starters. How many head do you have coming?"

That would refer to cattle, Daniel assumed. "How many do you think I should have?"

Toby gave him a look of pure disdain. "Don't you know anything?"

"Sure. But I'm new to the ranch business. I've got a lot to learn."

The boy shook his head in disgust. "You're telling me."

"Speaking of learning…" Daniel glanced at his watch. "It's noon on a Tuesday afternoon. Shouldn't you be in school?"

Scuffing the dirt floor with one toe, Toby avoided his eyes. "Nah."

"There's no school today?"

Hands in his jeans pockets, Toby shrugged, still staring at the ground.

"I guess that means you're playing hooky."

"What's that?"

"Skipping school. Cutting class."

"Oh." Another shrug, and then another sneeze. "School's useless."

"Why is that?"

"'Cause when I grow up I'm gonna run this ranch, just like my dad did. I don't need school for that. I can learn what I have to know staying home, working with my mom and the hands."

"Did your dad go to school?"

Toby looked up at him with a surprised expression. "I don't know." And sneezed again.

Daniel nodded. "You should ask your mom about that. I'll take you home so you can talk to her." He turned toward the barn door, but the boy hung back.

"She's gonna be mad."

"Probably. I imagine she likes to know where you are during the day."

Toby hung his head and sniffed. "I'm in big trouble."

After letting him anticipate the worst for a minute, Daniel put a hand on his shoulder to move him forward. "You might as well face the inevitable like a man. Get it over with."

"What's in-inevble?"

"Something you can't avoid."

"Oh." He sighed. Sneezed. "Yeah."

Once they were in the truck and headed back to Willa's house, Daniel said, "How'd you get out of going to school, anyway? Do your brother and sister know you're not there?"

"I said I was sick this morning. Once Robbie and Susannah left and Lili and Rosa were in the garden, I just went out the front door." He shrugged. "No big deal."

"Pretty slick." But Daniel had a feeling Willa would think it was a very big deal, indeed.

After a minute of silence, Toby said, "So what did you do to your leg?"

"My truck hit a landmine in Iraq." After eighteen months, he could say it without gritting his teeth.

Toby looked out the side window. "That's what happened to my dad." His voice was subdued. "He died."

"I know. I'm sorry. Three of my friends got killed when I was hurt."

After a minute, Toby glanced at the hand controls Daniel used to drive the truck. "Do you mind having a…a limp?"

An honest question deserved an honest answer. "Well, what would you think, if you couldn't play ball anymore—very well, anyway—or sit down easily, walk smoothly or stand up for a long time without your leg feeling like it was on fire?"

"I'd hate it."

"Sometimes I do. But at least I came home."

"You were lucky."

"Yeah, I was."

He could hear other questions seething in Toby's brain, but the boy didn't give voice to his thoughts. They rode down the driveway of the ranch house without another word. Once Daniel stopped the truck, Toby took a deep breath and wrapped his fingers around the door handle. "Thanks for the ride. I—"

Before he could finish, the door was yanked open from the outside. Willa stood there, clearly furious.

"Tobias Rafael Mercado, where have you been? What do you mean, sneaking off without telling anyone? You're not too old for a spanking, mister, and this may just be the day you get one."

She grabbed his arm and pulled him off the truck seat to stand in front of her. Bending down, she looked him straight in the eye. "Lili and Rosa have been worried sick, Toby. Why would you do something like this to them?"

Toby had adopted the toe-scuffing technique again. One shoulder lifted in a shrug.

Straightening up, Willa blew out a short breath. "We'll talk later. Go to your room…and stay there." The boy turned to start for the house, but she put a hand under his chin and made him look up at her. "Do you understand, Toby? Do not leave your room."

"Yes, ma'am." With a slump to his shoulders, dragging his feet, he went into the house. In the stillness of the day, the slam of a door could be heard clearly.

Willa stood for a moment with her shoulders hunched, too. Then she straightened up and looked at Daniel through the open truck door. "Where did you find him?" Her cheeks were bright red with what he figured was pure embarrassment.

"In the barn at my place. He was up in the loft, and he sneezed. Maybe he really does have a cold."

"If he was sick, he should have stayed home in bed instead of worrying my aunts to death."

"I guess so."

"He's been a handful recently. Always up to something." She said it almost to herself…or as if he were a friend she'd turned to for advice.

But Daniel knew she didn't want help from him. He put his hand on the key to crank the truck engine.

"Wait." Willa reached out, and he turned off the engine again. "I haven't said thank you."

"Not necessary."

"Of course it is. I appreciate you bringing him home—you saved us hours of worry."

"Anytime."

"I hope not." She flashed a smile that took him straight back to last night, to the incredible satisfaction he'd found with her. "I'll make sure he doesn't bother you again."

Daniel's mood crashed like a falling rock. "I'm sure you will." Once again he reached out to start the engine.

"Willa?" Two women came scurrying out the front door and across the veranda, both of them tiny, about sixty years old, with bright, dark eyes and identical faces. "Willa, we just talked to Toby. Is this Major Trent?"

"Yes, Lili. Daniel Trent." She gestured to the aunt wearing a pink-flowered dress. "Daniel, this is my aunt, Lilianna Mercado."

"Pleased to meet you," he said automatically, wishing he was outside and standing up instead of talking awkwardly across the interior of the truck.

The other aunt, wearing blue flowers, crowded in next to her sister. "This is Rosa Mercado," Willa said from behind them.

"Miss Rosa." Daniel nodded. "It's a pleasure."

"We're so grateful to you for bringing Toby home," Lili said. Rosa nodded in agreement. "He slipped away while we thought he was napping, and we had no idea where to look. And with Willa gone, we weren't at all sure what to do."

"It's no problem. I just found him in the barn and drove him back."

"We do appreciate your effort." Rosa put a hand on her chest, somewhere near her heart. "And we'd like to thank you properly. Please come in and join us for lunch."

Daniel glanced at Willa and saw her mouth tighten. "Thank you for the invitation, but it's really not necessary. I'll just get on back—"

"Oh, you can't!" Rosa leaned into the truck, bracing her hands on the passenger seat. "I'm sure you don't have much in the way of groceries up at that house, and it's so far to drive to the nearest town, you'll be starving before you get anything to

eat. Please, come in. Willa should have asked you before now."
She gave her niece a reproving look.

Trapped. While he was still trying to think of a way to say
no, Willa cleared her throat. "Lili and Rosa are right, Daniel.
Come in and have some lunch. It's the least we can do since you
brought Toby home."

His stomach chose that moment to growl fiercely, and the
Mercado sisters laughed. Lili clapped her hands. "You see, you
need some food right now. You're a big man. You shouldn't be
going hungry."

Daniel grinned and surrendered. "Who am I to argue with a
lovely woman? Thank you, Miss Lili. I'll be glad to stay for lunch."

Lili and Rosa fussed over him all the way into the house,
herding him through the large main room, with its twenty-foot
ceiling, into the dining room beyond, where they led him to the
head of an antique table that could easily have seated twenty
people. The chairs were equally old, ornately carved and uphol-
stered with red leather, but remarkably comfortable.

"You sit and relax—" Lili instructed, laying a hand lightly
on his shoulder "—while we get the food ready. It'll just be a
moment or two."

In little more than that, the table was spread with a lunch the
size of which Daniel had seldom seen outside an army mess hall.
He'd expected Mexican food, but instead there was a huge casserole pan of lasagna, with hot cheese and tomato sauce bubbling
on top, plus a crisp salad in a glass bowl, warm bread in a
napkin-lined basket, sliced apples and pears on a silver plate…

"This isn't lunch," he said when they joined him, the aunts
on his left and Willa on his right. "It's a banquet." He looked at
Willa. "Toby doesn't get to eat?"

"I took a plate to his room," she said, her eyes on the salad
she was serving herself. "He had fallen asleep. I guess he does
have a cold."

"I thought he had a slight fever when I touched his forehead this morning." Rosa shook her head. "But not enough to keep him in bed, I guess."

"Ten-year-old boys are pretty hard to tie down." Daniel forked up a bite of the lasagna. "Wow. Delicious."

Rosa and Lili smiled at his appreciative groan. Willa took a deep breath and let it out slowly, finally allowing herself to relax a little. She'd been afraid, though of what, she wasn't quite sure. She hadn't really thought Daniel would try to—to sweep her off her feet in her own home, in front of her aunts and her child. Despite what they'd done…together…last night…she didn't know him at all. But she believed she could trust him to behave in front of her family, at least.

Maybe she didn't trust herself?

She dropped her fork at the thought, and everyone looked up as it clattered against the china plate. "Sorry," she managed. "The lasagna is terrific, Lili. As always."

Focusing on her food again, she had to admit it was nice to have a man at the head of the table once more. Jamie had sat at the other end, nearest the kitchen, and Lili and Rosa had avoided putting Daniel in his seat. But the sheer size and presence of a strong, virile male made a difference in the room. A difference she had sorely missed.

And wasn't that just wonderful? Here she was, already putting Daniel Trent into her dead husband's place. This was just what she'd hoped to avoid, warning him off. They didn't need another man in their lives, stirring up hope in the kids, getting Lili and Rosa all flustered, making Willa herself wish for more of what she'd had last night. She'd simply have to resist any urge to get closer. How hard could that be?

Looking up just as he smiled at Lili after yet another compliment, she got an inkling of exactly *how* hard, indeed. The man was a charmer. And she was far from immune.

She couldn't help noticing he made a good meal—two helpings of lasagna and salad, three pieces of bread and even seconds on the flan Rosa brought out for dessert. Willa, on the other hand, found her appetite had deserted her. Her plate returned to the kitchen with most of the food untouched.

"That was quite a meal," he commented as she walked him back to the front door. "Please be sure your aunts know how much I appreciate their efforts."

"I think you made it clear." She opened the heavy door to the veranda and ushered him out ahead of her. "Anyway, they love having company. We haven't seen many guests in the past couple of years."

Standing in the shade, he turned to look at her, his blue gaze serious, his face solemn. "I'm sorry, Willa. I know this wasn't what you wanted."

She shook her head, then waved a hand in dismissal. "I'm the one who should apologize. I wasn't…nice…this morning."

"I don't expect you to be 'nice.' Honest is good."

"Okay, then." She pulled in a deep breath and took the risk of meeting his eyes. "Last night can't ever happen again. It wasn't—wasn't *me*. I can't afford to be so irresponsible. And the kids—they're still grieving—"

Daniel held up a hand. "It's okay. I get it." He put his weight on the cane and pivoted toward his truck. Once on the other side of the hood, he looked at her again.

"I'll keep my distance from you and your family," he promised. "You'll have to come looking if you want to find me. And, Willa…" That sexy, inviting grin curved his lips. "I can guarantee last night won't happen again—until *you* ask for it!"

"I LIKE THAT YOUNG MAN." Lili set a stack of dirty plates on the kitchen counter.

"I do, too." Rosa breathed in a lungful of steam as she filled the sink with soapy water. When they'd realized they would have a guest for lunch, they'd decided to use the second-best china, which had to be washed by hand. "He's very handsome."

"Oh, yes. He reminds me of…" Lili shook her head. "I think he'll be a good neighbor."

Rosa didn't have to hear the rest of the sentence to know whom her sister was thinking about. "Willa seems doubtful. And very disturbed by him."

"That's good, isn't it?"

"Could be. She's barely aware of poor Sheriff Sutton, no matter how hard he tries. But…" Rosa shook her head. "Willa's a stubborn one. Even if she couldn't resist falling for Major Trent, I doubt she'd admit it, to herself or anybody else."

"Do you think he's interested?"

"Oh, yes. There was a smile in his eyes every time he glanced at her."

"Well, he's our neighbor now, so I'm sure we'll be seeing quite a bit of him. He'll want Willa's advice on hiring hands, to start with."

Rosa paused in the act of sponging off a plate and stared out the window over the sink for a moment. "He'll need a foreman, too, won't he?"

"I expect so." Lili put the leftover lasagna in the refrigerator. "He did say he hadn't done much ranching."

"Yes. Yes, he did." And she might know just the man for the job. Biting back a smile, Rosa looked down into the suds again. "I'm sure Willa could make getting his ranch going much easier for Major Trent, if she wanted to."

Drying the plate Rosa had just washed, Lili wrinkled her forehead in distress. "Why wouldn't she want to?"

"She may take a while to get used to the idea of another man in her life." Rosa handed over the sparkling-clean fruit bowl and winked. "But when it comes to Major Trent, there's three of us and only one of her."

Lili's face cleared and she gave one of her delightful rippling laughs. "How true. Dear Willa doesn't stand a chance!"

Chapter Four

The van delivering Daniel's worldly possessions pulled into his driveway at nine o'clock Saturday morning. The Mercado kids arrived on horseback ten minutes later. They galloped up the road in a cloud of dust and slid to a stop on the bare dirt in front of the house. Toby sat on a sturdy brown-and-white horse with a friendly face. His sister—the image of her mother—rode a beautiful palomino with a dark gold coat and a cornsilk mane and tail, while the older boy seemed completely comfortable on his very tall, very black mount.

"Hi," Toby said, before sliding to the ground. "We came to help you move in. This is Robbie and Susannah. My horse is Patches. Suze rides Lustre, and Robbie's horse is Tar." He nodded toward his siblings. "We'll put them in the corral."

"Wait a minute." Daniel suppressed the smile he was feeling. "I don't recall asking for help."

"We're neighbors," Susannah said. "That's what we do."

He was pretty sure they hadn't checked with their mother before heading his way. And he didn't want to come between Willa and her children. "Well, you see those two big guys right there?" He waved his cane at the movers who were levering his new recliner out of the van. "They've got everything under control. I appreciate the offer, but I think you three had better head back to your house. You must have chores to do for your mom."

The shock and disappointment on their faces would have been comical, if he hadn't felt like such a heel turning them away. Toby stood with his jaw hanging loose, as if he couldn't believe what he'd heard. "But—"

"Come on, Toby." Robbie, who looked the least like his mother, with bigger bones and a fuller face, wheeled his horse. "We've got work to do at home. We don't have to stay where we're not wanted." He pressed his heels into the black horse's sides and took off at a fast lope. With a glance back at Daniel, Susannah shrugged and followed.

Toby threw his own disgusted look in Daniel's direction, pulled himself into the saddle and kicked his pony to a gallop. Daniel watched in admiration and a little envy as they charged back down the hill. All three kids rode like they were part of the animal underneath them.

That was why he was so shocked to see Toby's horse buck several times, then rear straight up on its hind legs—not once, but twice. The second time, Toby fell off.

Daniel heard one of the kids shout. By the time he had his truck backed out of the carport, he saw that Robbie and Susannah had returned to help their brother. A minute later, he stood beside Susannah as she knelt in the dirt with Toby. Robbie waited nearby, holding the three horses.

"He's knocked out," Susannah said, a thread of panic edging her voice. "I don't know what happened. He never falls."

Daniel mentally cursed his inability to get down on his knees. "Do cell phones work out here?" Susannah shook her head. He looked over at the older boy. "You have to go home and get your mother. If she can get a doctor to come, that's a good idea." The boy stared at him blankly. "Go on, Rob. Move it!"

The military tone worked. Robbie managed to mount his

horse while still holding the reins of the other two, and then set off down the road at a trot.

"Now, let's see what's with Toby." Daniel leaned as far as he could over the prone little boy. "Can you tell if he's broken a bone?"

Susannah felt up and down Toby's limbs and shook her head. "Nothing feels weird."

"Run your fingers over his scalp, under his hair. Any cuts? Bleeding?"

She did as instructed. If Daniel hadn't been watching closely, he'd have missed the wince that passed across Toby's face. Coupled with the good color in his cheeks and the even rise and fall of the boy's chest, that flinch suggested to Daniel that they might be dealing with injuries more pretended than real.

"Okay, then, let's check his ribs." Balancing on his cane, he reached down and tickled his fingers up and down Toby's rib cage. The little boy made a really valiant effort…but in the end, he had to laugh.

"Don't! Stop," he pleaded, giggling, and curled into a ball. "That—ouch!" The sudden gasp of pain was real. "It hurts!" He folded his arms over his midriff and opened his eyes. "Something really hurts."

"Show me where." When Toby put his fingertips on his rib cage, Daniel nodded. "You may have cracked that rib, big guy. Do you feel okay, otherwise? Headache? Dizzy? How many fingers am I holding up?"

"Three."

"Yep." Daniel straightened up, ignoring the scream of his own muscles. "Let's see if we can get you on your feet. Susannah, take his arm and I'll take the other hand." Carefully, they levered Toby to stand. "How's that feel?"

"Okay, 'cept I have this ache…" He curled his torso around his arms.

"Come lie down in the back of my truck. We'll wait for your

mom and I can drive you down to your house or the doctor, whichever she wants."

Toby climbed gamely into the backseat of the truck and even agreed to lay his head on Susannah's leg as she sat beside him.

"What happened?" She brushed a fringe of black hair off her brother's forehead. "What caused Patches to spook like that?"

"I dunno." Toby shrugged, then winced. "Maybe he saw a snake. A rattler, coiled up on the side of the road, ready to strike."

Susannah frowned. "I didn't see a snake when I went by."

"That doesn't mean there wasn't one."

"But the other horses—"

"Are stupid." Toby shoved himself away from his sister. "I said I don't know what happened."

"That's okay." Daniel touched Susannah's shoulder lightly. "We won't worry about why right now. You need to stay still, Toby. Lie back down."

But the boy had his lower lip stuck out and refused to relax. "Let's just go home."

"No, we'll get your mother here first." At the sound of an approaching engine, Daniel glanced down the road. "There she is, now."

Willa dropped down from her truck and strode toward Daniel. "Is he hurt?" Her dark eyes were fierce with worry.

"He might have cracked a rib. Otherwise, I think he's okay." He stepped back as she reached him, allowing her to peer into the backseat.

"Toby, what have you done this time?"

"Patches spooked and reared," Susannah said. "He says it was a snake on the road, but I don't believe him." She slid out, and Willa took her place next to Toby.

Robbie had come back with his mother, and he walked up while Willa talked to Toby. "Come on, Suze. Let's get in the truck. Mom wants to take him into town to the doctor."

She rolled her eyes at him. "Can't you be polite?" Then she looked at Daniel. "Thanks, Major Trent. I appreciate your help."

Daniel gave her a smile. "I'm glad I was close by."

Susannah smiled back and started to say something else, but Robbie grabbed her arm. "Come on." With a jerk, he got her started toward Willa's vehicle. She glanced back at Daniel and waved, before her brother urged her with both hands into the backseat. The door slammed shut. Despite the shadowed interior, Daniel saw the twins arguing.

Willa backed out of his truck and looked over. "You might be right. He'll need an X-ray, I guess."

"That's a good idea."

"Thanks again for taking care of him." Blowing out a deep breath, she tented her fingers against her lips for a moment. "I can't imagine what happened, though. Patches has always been bomb-proof—he never spooks. I've been on him when a snake actually crossed his path. On the other hand, Toby usually sticks like a burr. He's been riding his whole life."

Daniel decided to keep his thoughts to himself. "Maybe he was thinking about something else. I'm just glad he didn't hit his head."

"Me, too." Her gaze met his for a second. "Robbie said your furniture arrived."

"Yeah, what there is of it."

"They rode up to help you, I guess."

He nodded. "I doubted you knew they'd come over."

"No."

"So I sent them home."

Looking away from him, she nodded. "Um…I appreciate that. Now, we'll get out of your way, let you move in." She walked quickly to the other side of the truck, helped Toby out and led him to her vehicle with an arm around his shoulders. Once behind the wheel again, she gave Daniel a wave, echoed by Toby and Susannah, then executed a precise three-point turn and headed back down the hill in a cloud of dust.

Daniel returned to his house to find that the movers, with no direction, had deposited his bedroom furniture in the living room and were ready to be on their way. He offered them fifty bucks in cash to assemble the bed where it belonged and place the dresser and chest of drawers that had belonged to his great-grandmother. Gritting his teeth, he also requested them to unstack the boxes so he could open each one without having to lift. Then, embarrassed, he let them leave.

Sitting in his recliner a few minutes later, he heard the distinct sound of a car engine shutting off outside his door. When he'd levered himself to stand and reached the living room window, he could see that an ancient station wagon—the kind with real wood panels on the sides—had pulled into the yard. As he watched, one of the Mercado ladies came around to the back and lowered the tailgate, at the same time as someone knocked on the door.

The other aunt stood there, as he'd expected. "Good afternoon," she said brightly. "Lili and I thought you would need some help getting settled. If you'll hold open the door, we'll bring these things inside."

He'd had trouble telling the twins apart at lunch. Now he noticed that Rosa wore a metal bracelet, the kind used to remember prisoners of war and soldiers missing in action. That would help him keep them straight. "Miss Rosa, you don't have to…"

His protest fell on deaf ears. She went back to the wagon and collected a big basket, as Lili approached carrying a cardboard box. "Hello, again, Major Trent. These go to the kitchen."

"Miss Lili, I can't let you—"

She, too, ignored him. And so Daniel stood there, bemused, as the two ladies paraded back and forth from house to wagon, carting in groceries and he didn't know what else.

"That's all," Lili said, as she came in again. "You can close the door now. We've let out enough of the cool air." When Daniel followed her into the kitchen, he found Rosa unpacking pots and pans.

"We weren't sure whether you had kitchen supplies," she told him. "And I gather, looking at your boxes, that you don't."

"Um…no." Daniel ran a hand through his hair. "I haven't cooked much, over the years."

"That's quite all right. We have plenty to spare."

"And dishware?" Lili lifted a stack of plates out of a box. "Do you have your own?"

He shook his head. "You really shouldn't have—"

Lili waved away his objections. "We didn't expect a bachelor to have much in the way of provisions. So we brought some basics. And some frozen meals, to get you started. Those are already in the freezer."

The freezer, Daniel saw when he opened the door, was filled with neatly labeled packages. "Your lasagna," he said weakly. "That was really good." He'd been eating peanut butter sandwiches since that one great lunch at Willa's house.

"And, of course, you're welcome to any meal at our house," Lili said. "Even breakfast, if you want to drive down that early. You don't have to call—just arrive and we'll feed you."

"Thanks." Daniel could just imagine Willa's face if he showed up for breakfast, or any other meal, unannounced and uninvited by her.

"Now, we'll get the sheets on your bed." Rosa headed for the bedroom. "And some towels in the bath."

"Ladies…" Daniel trailed after them. "I can make the bed. You really don't have to do all this work."

Again, his protests fell on deaf ears. The sisters set up his bed and bath to their satisfaction, all the way down to unwrapping the bars of soap for sink and shower. When they started eyeing the boxes, however, Daniel took charge.

"No," he said firmly, "you aren't going to unpack for me. I couldn't live with myself if I let you work so hard. You've already done too much."

"Nonsense." Lili allowed him to escort her back to the living room. "You've saved Toby twice, now—we couldn't possibly do too much."

"Then we'll call it even." Daniel surveyed them both. "But it's getting late and you'll want to be back home before dark."

He was able to help them into the wagon one-handed, and then stepped back. "Thank you for everything. You're welcome to visit anytime—come empty-handed, though!"

They laughed and beeped the horn. Daniel watched them out of sight down the road before going back into his house.

His *well-provisioned* house, now that the Mercado sisters had been there. Between the luxury of choosing whether to enjoy beef stew or meat loaf for dinner, the prospect of a good night's sleep on cool, smooth sheets and a swig from one of the beers Rosa had stowed in his refrigerator, Daniel felt as if he'd finally come home.

He raised his bottle in a toast. "To the New Moon Ranch," he said aloud. "Willa, my dear, you'll just have to learn to like losing!"

TOBY WANTED HIS MOM NEARBY while the doctors examined him, but Robbie and Susannah were told to remain in the waiting room.

"I hope he's not really hurt." Susannah hunched her shoulders and hugged her arms around her waist.

Robbie propped his elbows on his knees and stared at his hands. "Yeah, well, he deserves it, pulling a stunt like that."

"What stunt?"

"You are so gullible." He threw his sister an impatient look. "He made Patches rear, then deliberately fell off."

"Oh." She was quiet for a few seconds. "Why would he do that?"

"'Cause he's all excited about Major Daniel Trent from the U.S. Army. He wanted that Trent dude to come to the rescue." He used a sissy voice to make the title sound as silly as possible.

"He's a nice man, Robbie. I like his smile."

"You would."

She punched him in the shoulder. "I'm not stupid."

"Sure you are," he said, just to make her mad. Then he grinned, so she'd know he didn't mean it.

After she stuck out her tongue at him, Susannah said, "Why do you think Toby's so interested in Major Trent?"

"Duh? Because it's like Dad coming back again?"

She didn't say anything. When he looked around, she'd bowed her head over her arms, and he saw a tear splash on her wrist. After a minute, though, she sniffed and straightened up. "So you think Toby wants Major Trent to take Daddy's place?"

Robbie shrugged one shoulder.

"Marry Mom, and everything?"

"Don't make me gag. Mom doesn't need another husband. She's got us to take care of her."

"She's pretty lonely. So maybe—" Susannah stared at him, her eyebrows wrinkled. "Would that make him our dad?"

"Nope."

"And would he run the ranch? Would he…would he own it, once he married Mom?"

"I—I don't think so." Robbie could still hear in his head what his dad had said, kneeling in front of him just before he got on the plane. *"I'm counting on you, son. Take care of your mom. And take care of the Blue Moon."*

Susannah tugged on his sleeve. "Robbie, are you sure?"

Robbie realized he'd closed his eyes. He opened them wide and saw his mom and Toby emerge from the examination area across the room. "The Blue Moon belongs to the Mercados,

Suze." He made his voice strong, so she'd believe him. "Always has, always will."

He'd make sure of that, somehow. For his dad's sake.

NIGHT HAD FALLEN BY THE TIME Willa pulled her truck into the driveway at the house. She cut the engine, climbed out and went to help Toby off the high seat.

"I don't need help," he complained, but then leaned heavily on her hand as he came to the ground.

"I know you don't. But humor me—moms like to help when their kids have cracked ribs."

"Okay." He pulled free soon enough and walked into the house under his own steam, but with a tired slump to his shoulders.

"He doesn't feel good." Susannah came up on Willa's right. "Maybe they should have put him in the hospital."

"He's just begging for sympathy," Robbie countered. "You watch—he'll want extra dessert because he's hurt."

"I think he's sore," Willa told them. "But maybe he's learned a lesson." They both looked at her in question and she shrugged. "My guess is he tried to fall off…and succeeded better than he expected."

Susannah held out her hands in a helpless gesture. "But why?"

"I told you. 'Cause he wanted to stay with his new hero," Robbie said with disgust. "He's all hung up over the Trent guy."

"That's Major Trent to you." Willa gave him a severe look. "Be respectful. He's an officer in the Army and was wounded in the service of this country."

Her son hunched his shoulders. "Yeah, yeah. Why should he have come back, when…" Abruptly, without finishing the thought, he turned on his heel and headed away from the kitchen door, around the corner of the house.

"Dinner's going to be ready," Willa called after him. "Don't stay out long." She sighed when he didn't answer.

Susannah put a hand on her shoulder. "I'll get him." She took off after her twin at an easy jog.

Alone in the twilight, Willa seized the opportunity to sit down on the courtyard wall and catch her breath. The day had been hectic even before Robbie had come riding up to report Toby's accident. Two cowboys had quit on her this morning, demanding back pay that stretched her cash flow to its limit. Her foreman, Jorge Ramirez, had reported that at least fifty head of cattle were missing, thanks no doubt to the rustlers working out of the desert. She'd called the sheriff, *again,* but there wasn't much he could do after the fact and he didn't have the manpower to police her fence line every night.

Added to those concerns, worry and tension over Toby had taken their toll as she and the kids made the long trip into the hospital and waited for a doctor's verdict. On the way back, which seemed even longer, she'd wrestled with thoughts about Daniel Trent.

She couldn't believe it, but in the midst of her anxiety this morning, she had again noticed the man's sheer physical appeal. His black T-shirt had revealed the contoured muscles of his arms and chest, while slim-fitting, well-worn jeans had showcased his long legs. Even knowing how the skin under his clothes had been ravaged, she'd found herself stirred all over again by the shape and proportions of his body.

And then there was his smile, his concerned blue gaze, the reassurance in his rich voice. So tempting, that ice-cream sundae voice. She remembered how he'd said her name as he'd touched her skin, as he'd moved inside of her…

"Willa?" Rosa spoke from the open door to the kitchen. "What in the world are you doing out here in the dark? Dinner is ready."

"Coming." She could only hope the night air would cool the heat in her face generated by memories of Daniel Trent.

After dinner, she went to her office to work on the ranch accounts. All too often, however, her concentration faltered, until she threw her pencil across the room in disgust.

Somehow, she had to keep Daniel out of her thoughts. He represented her biggest mistakes—breaking up the Blue Moon and allowing herself to be swept off her feet by a stranger's sexy grin.

The first mistake would be corrected in three months. Maybe less, when Daniel realized that he simply couldn't cope with the physical demands of ranching. She'd get that land parcel back, and she'd be sure to keep tight hold of it for the rest of her life. Of course she could use the money from the sale—who couldn't use almost a million dollars? But the earnest money he'd already paid would help satisfy the most pressing of her current debts.

As a means of encouraging herself, Willa took out a red marker and crossed off the past five days on her big desk pad calendar. Then she turned to the page for December and put a circle around the box for the twenty-first, adding two dots for eyes and an arc for the mouth. A smiling face now looked up at her, marking the day Daniel Trent would be gone.

Her second mistake couldn't be so easily edited. If it were simply a case of forgetting the night she'd spent with a stranger, she'd have dealt with the guilt and moved on. But the ease with which she'd succumbed to her desire for Daniel reminded Willa of her backseat tryst sixteen years ago with a boy who'd treated her like dirt afterward.

I'll keep my distance, she promised herself as she turned back to her bookkeeping. *And I'll make sure he keeps his.*

Eighty-three days. I can last that long. Eighty-three days to December 21…and counting.

Chapter Five

Daniel had just started on his first cup of Monday morning coffee when the doorbell rang. He was wearing the sweatpants and T-shirt he'd slept in, but this surely couldn't be Lili and Rosa Mercado. Not so early.

Still, he looked through the window before opening the door. The man standing on his front stoop was on the short side, bow-legged and deeply tanned, with lines in his face from age and the sun. His dusty boots, frayed, faded jeans, and red, long-sleeved shirt with a blue bandana at the throat epitomized the word *cowboy*.

"You gonna open the door?" he called. "I can smell the coffee out here."

Grinning, Daniel did as requested. "Good morning."

The man tipped his standard-issue white cowboy hat. "'Morning. I'm Nate Hernandez. Heard you need a ranch foreman."

"Where did you hear that?" Daniel hadn't yet figured out the best way to go about advertising for help.

"Rosa Mercado mentioned it at church yesterday. Sure could use a cup of coffee."

Of course. With a fatalistic shrug, Daniel stepped back. "Come on in. Help yourself."

"Thanks." Nate went straight to the kitchen, found the correct cupboard and pulled out a mug. Only after a couple long draws on the coffee did he look at Daniel again. "I got plenty of references. I worked for the Mercados and other ranchers in the area. Ain't nothing much needs doing on a ranch I ain't done or cain't do."

"Where are you working now?"

"I been retired for a few years."

"So why do you want to work for me?"

A tinge of red brightened the dark complexion. "Miss Rosa asked."

"Ah." Daniel nodded. "She's a persuasive lady."

"That, she is."

They drank to the bottoms of their mugs in silence. After pouring a refill for them both, Daniel cleared his throat. "I won't deny I need the help. I did some ranch work as a teenager, and I've done a lot of reading but—"

"Ain't the same as doing it."

"No."

"You got a bum leg, too, I hear."

"Yeah. And some back problems."

Nate nodded. "Need to be careful about the horse you ride. Some'll take care of you, some won't. Plus, you'll need a crew doing the ground work for you."

"Do you know a few guys who need jobs?"

"I think I can round up some decent hands. How much you paying?"

"What's the going rate?"

By the time they'd finished their second cup of coffee, Daniel and Nate had struck a mutually agreeable deal. They talked for the rest of the morning about starting up the New Moon operation. Nate knew of a rancher in Jim Hogg County who was selling off equipment and cattle and whom Nate thought would give Daniel a fair deal. "We can take a ride over there this afternoon, see what he's got."

"Sounds good." Daniel brought two steaming bowls of stew to the kitchen table. "I appreciate getting the benefit of your experience."

With his mouth already full, Nate waved his spoon in dismissal of the gratitude. "This is Miss Lili's stew, ain't it?"

"They brought me some frozen meals to get me started."

The foreman nodded. "Those two women are the best cooks in the county. Maybe in the state of Texas." He spooned up another mouthful but sighed instead of eating. "Lucky's the man who could persuade one of them to cook for him full-time."

"As a job, you mean?"

"Nah." Nate finished his bowl and went to the stove for seconds. "You'd have to marry her to get her to leave the Blue Moon."

Daniel hid his smile. "Did you ever ask?"

"Nah," Nate said again. "A Mercado wouldn't look at the likes of me. They're blue bloods, you know? I'm just a cowpoke." The regret in his rough voice kept Daniel silent.

With his stew finished and his bowl rinsed, Nate returned to business. "What we're gonna do now is find you a horse. Lotsa ranchers do their work with trucks and ATVs and such—even airplanes—but I hold that a man should be able to ride if he needs to and is able."

Daniel pushed out of his chair. "Well, I don't know about the *able* part, but I'm willing to try."

"You just need the right animal, careful and smart. I expect Willa's got one that'll do. She's a wonder at breaking and training a good horse."

"You want me to buy a horse from Willa Mercado?"

"You got a problem with that?"

"No, but she might."

Nate clucked his tongue and shook his head. "Don't believe it—she'll take good money like anybody else. Let's get down there, see what she's got for sale."

The expression on Willa's face when Daniel parked his truck near her horse barn a few minutes later proved him right. The line between her arched eyebrows, the downward tilt of those wide, soft lips, plainly said he wasn't welcome.

Nate ignored the message. He moseyed over to where she stood by the gate to a corral. "'Afternoon, Miss Willa. We came to look at some horses."

She glanced at Daniel, who was following Nate, then looked at the other man again. "You're helping him buy horses?"

"I'm his new foreman. We're getting his operation set up, and I figured you'd have a mount he could depend on."

If anything, her frown deepened. "You're working as foreman on the New Moon Ranch?"

"Yes, ma'am." Nate's attention had gone to the horses standing quietly inside the corral. "I like the look of that buckskin, there."

But Willa wouldn't be diverted. "You worked on the Blue Moon for twenty years, Nate."

His dark gaze swung back to hers. "Yes, ma'am, I did. Then Mr. Mercado, may he rest in peace, fired me. I'm sure you remember that." When Willa started to speak, Nate raised a hand. "Now, I ain't harboring hard feelings. What's past is past. I heard Major Trent, here, needed some help. I was getting tired of listening to myself think and thought I might as well be doing something useful. So tell me about the buckskin. How's he go?"

Willa blew out a deep breath. "He's hot," she said, exaggerating only a little. "Needs an experienced rider."

"Okay, how 'bout the black-and-white pinto gelding on the rail? I like the look in his eyes."

She did, too. She'd been thinking about keeping him for herself, since her favorite horse, Montezuma, was turning twenty-two next year. He couldn't keep working forever, and the pinto would make a dependable cow pony.

But selling meant one less horse to feed this winter. The price would easily cover the wages she'd paid out on the weekend. "He might be a good choice," she conceded, avoiding Daniel's blue eyes. "Real smart, easy gaits, no tricks. I like him."

Nate nodded. "Let's put a saddle on him."

She called Robbie, who brought a saddle and bridle out of the barn. Nate tacked up the pinto without fuss, then pulled himself easily onto the horse's back and proceeded to put him through his paces.

"He's good," Daniel commented, coming up beside Willa as she propped her arms on the fence.

"Nate spent years on the rodeo circuit." She didn't look at him, but she could feel his size, his warmth next to her. "He can ride anything with legs."

"I tried to tell him you wouldn't want to sell a horse to me."

Willa risked a glance at his face and found that grin waiting for her. She fought the urge to smile back and won, barely. "As long as you take care of him, I don't have a problem selling you the horse."

"Nice mover," Nate said, pulling up beside her at the fence. He swung his leg over the saddlehorn and slid to the ground. "Major Trent, have a go."

Willa, watching closely, saw Daniel swallow hard. "Sure," he said, leaning his cane against the fence post. "What's his name?"

"Calypso," she stuttered. "We call him Cal."

Inside the fence, Daniel circled to Cal's left side and put a hand on the gelding's neck. "Hey, there, Calypso. How's it going?"

"We'll take him out in the middle." Nate headed the horse away from the fence. "Give you more room to mount."

"Yeah, right." The soft comment came from Robbie, who'd joined Willa at the fence. "You might as well call the ambulance now, Mom. This won't be pretty."

"Hush." Her urge to defend Daniel surprised her. "He's ridden before."

"Cal will take care of him," Susannah said from Willa's other side. "He's a good horse."

Toby squeezed in between Willa and Robbie but didn't say a word as Daniel took the reins in one hand and put the other hand on the back of the saddle.

"We've got a mounting block," Willa called. "We can bring it out…"

Daniel gave a single shake of his head. His knuckles tightened at the rim of the saddle, and his shoulders lifted on a deep breath. He bent his left knee.

Toby said, "That's not how—"

Daniel gave an awkward jump, which somehow landed him on his stomach in the saddle, with both legs dangling on the horse's left side. As they watched, he fumbled for the stirrup with his left foot. Willa caught her breath—Cal wasn't used to this kind of mounting technique. Would he stand still?

Nate had hold of the bridle and reins, but Calypso sidled several steps under Daniel's weight. Willa didn't know whether to offer help or simply watch disaster unfold.

"Mom…" Susannah gripped her arm. "He's going to fall."

"I told you," Robbie said.

But then Daniel's boot slipped into the stirrup. Using the extra support, he straightened his arms, as in a push-up, over the horse's back. With Calypso fidgeting underneath him, he swung his stiff right leg from the hip—up, up and over the horse's hindquarters. Finally, he lowered his seat carefully onto the saddle.

Willa thought her knees might collapse in relief. Daniel leaned forward and patted Calypso on the side of the neck. "Good boy," he said. "We're going to get along fine."

Nate spent a minute adjusting the right stirrup to accommodate Daniel's stiff leg, then stepped back with his hands on his hips. "Take him for a spin."

Daniel grinned. "Not literally, I hope." First at a walk, then a jog and a lope, he rode Calypso around the corral—not always in balance, not completely in control, but Cal's good manners made up for what his rider lacked in technique.

Robbie turned away from the fence. "It'll happen," he predicted. "Hope somebody's there to pick up the pieces. Come on, Suze. We gotta finish cleaning the stalls."

"I'm coming." Susannah started to follow but looked back just as Willa glanced her way. There was no mistaking the stars in the girl's eyes. She'd contracted a serious case of hero worship.

Terrific, Willa thought. *That makes two of them.*

Daniel dismounted with more speed and less effort than he'd needed to get on and led the horse back to Willa without Nate's help. "I think Cal and I can work together." He rubbed the pinto's nose. "I guess we'll be buying a horse trailer sometime this week and we'll pick up Calypso then, if that works for you."

"Sure." Watching him walk away with Nate, she thought she saw the toll his ride had taken in the way he leaned on the cane. How would he manage the daily grind of ranch work, if a few minutes in the saddle took such effort?

"He's really strong," Toby said in an awed voice. "Trick riders do stuff like that."

"Sometimes." The silver truck disappeared toward the main road in a cloud of dust. For the first time since Daniel arrived, Willa felt like she could breathe easily.

Toby followed her toward the barn. "I've ridden Cal. I could help him."

"Nate works for Major Trent, Toby. He doesn't need our help."

"But—"

"You've got your own chores to do here, plus homework. When do you have time to help anybody else?"

She reached the barn door, only to realize that Toby had stopped quite a distance behind her. "Are you coming?" she asked. "I want to check the fence line in the south pasture. We can take Patches and Monty out for an afternoon run."

He shook his head. "I have homework." Turning on his heel, her son stalked in the direction of the house, leaving Willa with no doubt of what he thought about her reasons for being a bad neighbor.

And the really sad thing, she thought as she saddled her horse, *is that he's absolutely right.*

SHORTLY AFTER SUNRISE on Tuesday, Daniel had just nailed up a new board to replace one of the broken pieces in the corral when he heard the sound of hoofbeats coming up the road. He straightened his back, groaning a little, to see Rob Mercado approach on his tall black horse, with Calypso jogging close behind.

"Good morning." Daniel lifted a hand in greeting. "You didn't have to deliver Cal—we would have come to get him."

"My mom told me to bring him up here." Rob held out Cal's lead rope, and Daniel limped over to take the horse. Looking around, the boy shook his head. "You sure got a lot of work to do."

"That's right," Nate said, coming out of the barn. "And we could use some strong young muscles like yours to help us. What do you say? Want to earn some extra cash?"

Rob's eyes brightened at the word *cash,* but then his face fell. "I've got school. Besides, you're hiring some hands, aren't you?"

"Won't start till next week. The corrals as they stand ain't safe enough for this nice horse." He took Calypso's lead rope from Daniel. "Major Trent and me can get it done, but the job'd go faster with some extra hands."

Daniel kept quiet—he figured any effort he made at persuasion would only drive the boy away. After considering for a minute, Rob nodded. "I guess I could come for a couple of hours after school. But I have to get my chores at home done, too. I can't stay late." He threw Daniel a defiant glance.

"No problem." Daniel shrugged. "An hour or two will be a big help. Thanks for bringing the horse."

Rob cleared his throat. "You're welcome." Once back in the saddle, he gave a brief wave. "See you later." With a movement of his heels, the black horse leapt into a ground-shaking gallop, which gradually faded away.

"He's a good boy," Nate said. "I hear he's had a hard time since his daddy was killed."

"I think they all have." Daniel lowered himself to sit on a bale of straw. "Losing a father…a husband…isn't something you get over quickly."

"Jamie Mercado was a decent man. Not the steadiest, maybe…" The foreman shrugged.

Daniel knew Willa would hate being the subject of gossip. But maybe Nate could help him understand her better. "Not steady, how?"

"He liked speculating—invested in some crazy projects over the years. Willa only found out about a couple of them after he died and the money wasn't there for paying the bills."

"Hmm." So Willa's husband had left her in debt. Yet she felt she owed it to him to keep the ranch together and felt guilty for selling part of it. If she couldn't trust her own husband, how would she ever trust a stranger? "So, do we have a place to park Calypso until I can get these boards nailed up?"

"I'll tie him up with some hay for the time being." Nate accepted the change of subject with a nod. "He'll be good till we're done."

True to his word, Rob arrived about three-thirty each afternoon for the rest of the week and worked hard for two solid hours without protest or complaint. Daniel didn't ask if Willa had objected to the arrangement and the boy didn't volunteer any information.

The three of them didn't really talk much at all. Daniel needed most of his strength for the work itself and to force his body to cooperate. He took as few breaks as possible, especially while Rob was present, and went to bed dead-tired at night.

Thursday, though, Rob looked over at him while they waited for Nate to cut a board for the side of the barn. "You went to Iraq, like my dad."

"That's right."

"Did you fight in many battles?"

"I saw my share."

"What's it like?"

Daniel debated his answer for a moment. "Loud. Hot. Dirty and confusing. Scary."

Rob curled his lip. "You were scared?"

"I don't know anybody who wasn't. You look death in the face, then follow orders, anyway. That's a soldier's job."

The boy nodded. "I guess so. What kind of stuff did you do?"

"Well..." Daniel sifted through his memories, trying to find some that were G-rated. "We helped build two schools and a hospital. I did some mentoring for Iraqi kids, coached soccer for a couple of teams—"

Rob dismissed those efforts with a snort. "Did you hunt down terrorists?"

"Yeah, I did."

"Did you kill any of them?"

"When I had to." Too often.

"How many? Did you get medals and stuff?" The boy's eyes glowed with excitement. He raised his arms as if he held a rifle and mimicked the sound of weapon fire, jerking the imaginary gun with each shot. "Pow. Pow, pow, pow. Pow."

Daniel sliced his straight arm down across the boy's hands. "War is a terrible experience, Rob. Don't ever take it lightly."

They were still staring at each other when Nate came back with the board. Daniel excused himself from the nailing process and returned to the house, where he sat for a long time in the dark, thinking about all the buddies he'd lost to war. Including one he'd never met…Jamie Mercado.

By sundown on Friday, the corrals and the cattle pens were in good shape—clean, repaired and functional. Daniel handed Rob a crisp fifty-dollar bill. "I appreciate the effort. Anytime you want to come around, we'll have work for you."

Rob's eyes went round in his dirty, sweat-streaked face. "Wow…thanks!"

"Thank you." Daniel swiped at his forehead with his shirt sleeve—the October weather in south Texas resembled his memories of summer in Ohio. "Have you got time for one more quick chore?"

Still staring at the fifty, the boy said, "Sure."

Daniel led the way into the house, where three moving boxes still sat in the living room. "Would you help me move these into the bedroom?"

Rob squatted beside a box as if to lift it on his own, but couldn't get it off the floor. "Man, that's heavy. What's in there?"

"Army gear," Daniel said, carefully casual. "Boots, uniforms, junk I carried around with me. I'll get the other side."

Despite Daniel's aching back, the two of them moved the three containers into a corner of the bedroom. Each time they set down a box, the clank of metal hinted at the true nature of the contents. Daniel ignored the sounds, and Rob didn't ask for an explanation.

At the front door, Daniel handed the boy an extra ten dollars. "Thanks again, Rob. Can you ride your pony home in the dark?"

Without meeting his eyes, Rob shrugged one shoulder. "Sure."

He called Willa a little while later just to check. "And I wanted to thank you for letting him help out. Nate and I are grateful."

"Rob made the choice," she said stiffly. "He had to work after dinner all week to get his chores here done, and then stay up late with his homework."

"He must have big plans for the money," Daniel joked. "What's he got his eye on—a new video game?"

Willa didn't say anything for a long time. "He wanted to share it with Susannah and Toby for lunch money. He heard me talking to Lili and Rosa about the bills and decided I can't afford to buy his school lunch."

Then she cut the connection without another word.

Chapter Six

After practicing with Calypso in one of the corrals all week, Daniel welcomed Nate's suggestion for a Saturday ride across the pasture land of the New Moon. A portable mounting block made getting into the saddle much less of a chore, and they set out midmorning armed with a map, a sack of sandwiches and a thermos of coffee.

They came across the first break in the fence about an hour later. Nate hopped off his sorrel pony, Daze, and went to inspect the wire.

"Cut." Stepping outside the ranch boundary, he examined the ground beyond the fence. "Hoofprints." He frowned in disgust. "ATV tracks. Damn rustlers."

"Rustlers?" Daniel sat up straight. "In the twenty-first century?"

"Bet your beef on it." Nate came back to his horse. "There's a good market over in Mexico for beef, with no questions asked about the brand or the source."

"So somebody's been rustling Mercado cattle, is that what you're saying?"

"Yep."

Daniel registered the sense of a big empty space where his guts used to be. Not only did he have to learn the ranching business from the ground up, but he had to deal with cattle thieves, too? Was he really up to the challenge? "Does Willa know about this?"

Nate shrugged one shoulder. "I expect she does. Come to think of it, I heard the sheriff mention something about rustlers out this way a few weeks ago. Miss Willa would've reported the theft, wouldn't she?"

"That would make sense." Daniel stifled his first impulse, which was to ride—what was the expression…hell for leather?—back to the Blue Moon and confront Willa about the rustling immediately. "Do you think this is the only break in the fence?"

In the course of the day, they discovered two more points where the wire had been cut, plus four places where the line had been dragged down by the cattle themselves. They made note of the locations, so the hands could ride out on Monday and start making repairs.

"We'll get this taken care of before the cattle arrive," Nate assured him. "Looks like the pasture and the water holes are in good shape otherwise. That rainstorm we had coupla weeks ago really did some good for the grass."

"Glad to hear it." Daniel avoided thinking about the storm, and the night with Willa, as much as possible. Fortunately, he worked so hard most days that he fell into bed too exhausted even to dream…well, except for those early mornings when he awoke sweating and stiff with desire, and the fragrance of Willa's hair was as real to him as the sheet clenched in his fists.

Back at the barn in the late afternoon, he helped Nate settle the horses for the night, said goodbye to his foreman until Monday morning and gave himself the luxury of a long, hot shower. Then, cleaned up but no less furious than he had been at eleven that morning, he drove his truck down to the Mercado house and stopped in the drive.

Rosa greeted him at the front door. "Why, Major Trent, what

a pleasure to see you! Please, come in." She led the way into the main parlor, with its high ceiling, gold-framed paintings and more of the dark wood furniture with leather upholstery that he'd seen in the dining room.

"Is Willa here?"

"I believe she came in a few minutes ago. Dinner will be ready in about half an hour. Can I persuade you to stay?"

He thought of what he had to say to her niece. "Thanks, Miss Rosa, but I…I'm going into town when I leave here. Another time, maybe."

Her eyebrows drew together in disappointment. "That's too bad. I hope you can join us soon. Have a seat and I'll find Willa for you."

Daniel didn't sit down, but browsed the pictures on the walls, instead. He was examining the recent portrait of a handsome man in a National Guard uniform—Jamie Mercado, he was sure—when footsteps approached on the tile floor of the entry hall.

He turned to find Willa standing in the doorway. "Daniel? I'm surprised to see you." Her tone was startled but not unfriendly. She even smiled a little.

The sight of her was enough to weaken his resolve. He didn't want to fight with Willa Mercado. He wanted to make her laugh, to hold her hand and kiss those wide, soft lips.

Then he gave himself a mental kick in the butt: "I was surprised, myself, when Nate and I found evidence this morning that rustlers have been stealing your cattle."

Willa stepped forward to grip the back of a chair. "I—"

"I can understand your reluctance to sell off part of the Blue Moon. I gave up expecting a neighborly welcome, and you did warn me not to look to you for help."

Even from across the room, he could see her cheeks flush bright red at the memory.

"But I had a right to know about the rustlers, Willa. You should have told me my cattle would be at risk on that property. Anyone I hire to work for me is in danger if we decide to interfere and these misfits play rough. By any standard, you owed me a warning. What the hell were you thinking?"

Willa rounded the chair, dropped onto the seat and covered her face with her hands. "I—I didn't expect you to move so fast. I thought you would take more time to get your crew, set up your operation."

"So you were planning to tell me at some point?"

She looked up and nodded. "Of course. I hoped having somebody on the northern side of the ranch would create a buffer between the Blue Moon and the rustlers. I'd planned to work with the owner, get the sheriff involved, see if we couldn't catch them in the act…"

"Using somebody else's herd as bait, right?" Daniel sat down in the chair directly across a low table from her. "And then you found out your new owner was a cripple."

"No! I didn't think about it like that." Willa pounded her fists on the arms of the chair. "I'm sorry—I should have told you sooner. But there's so much to do, to consider… I'm still getting used to the idea of that land belonging to somebody else. And after what happened—"

She stopped, a horrified expression on her face, and looked behind her as if she expected to see the whole family standing there, listening.

"Nobody's there." At another time, he might have smiled at her concern. Today he was just too damn mad.

A deep breath lifted her slim shoulders. "I didn't mean to put you in danger. We moved our cattle, and I thought it would be weeks, maybe months, before you had your own."

"Actually, what you think is that I won't be there past Christmas."

Her gaze dropped away from his. "I *hoped* the rustlers would give up, go prey on someone else. I was going to tell you. Soon."

"But you have alerted the sheriff?"

"The first time I realized I was missing cattle. He can't spare staff to patrol the perimeter full-time. Unless we catch them red-handed…" She shrugged. "I don't have a big enough crew for that kind of duty. The rustlers pretty much have the run of the desert."

"We'll see about that." His anger vented, Daniel felt fatigue wash over him. "I don't intend to contribute to their life-style."

"But—" she stood up as he got to his feet "—what are you going to do?"

He shrugged. "I don't have a plan, yet. Only intentions."

She gazed at him doubtfully. Daniel couldn't resist reaching out to stroke his fingertips along her cheek. "I'll be okay," he said quietly.

For a second, she submitted to his touch. Then her shoulders stiffened and her chin came up. "I'm sure you will. If you need some of my cowboys, let me know and we'll see what we can work out." Turning on her heel, she headed for the front door, clearly expecting him to follow.

"Your aunt invited me for dinner," he told her as he crossed the entry hall. At her look of dismay, he laughed aloud. "Don't worry, Willa. I said no, thanks."

As he reached her, standing by the open door, he paused. "But you can't avoid me forever. There's more between us than just a sales contract. Someday, we're going to have to figure out exactly what it is." Leaning closer, he pressed a quick kiss to her temple. "Someday soon."

He walked through the doorway and let her shut him outside without a goodbye. Standing on the veranda in the deepening twilight, Daniel thought about his brave last words.

And wondered if he stood a snowball's chance in hell of making them come true.

WILLA LEANED BACK AGAINST the closed door and commanded her heart to stop pounding. *Someday soon,* he'd said. But she didn't want to know what these feelings were between them. Once burned, twice shy, so the saying went. Well, she'd been burned twice now, and she'd learned to stay as far away as possible from the fire.

Before she could catch her breath, the quick tap of heels on tile announced Lilianna's arrival. "Where is Major Trent? Rosa said he'd arrived."

"He had to leave. I'm sure he's sorry he missed you." She started for the back of the house, but Lili stopped her with a hand on her arm.

"Couldn't you persuade him to stay for dinner?"

"I didn't try, Lili. He told Rosa he couldn't stay."

"Oh, but he was just being polite." Her aunt-in-law gave her a disapproving look. "And you, I'm afraid, were not. Where have your manners gone, Willa? You treat Major Trent like a—a criminal, instead of the personable, attractive neighbor he is."

"Just because I don't invite him to run tame in the house doesn't mean I'm being impolite."

"You can be friends with Major Trent, Willa, and still respect Jamie's memory. You don't have to be afraid—"

"I'm not afraid!" Her denial was all the more violent for being a lie. "He'll be gone by Christmas, Lili. I don't want the children getting attached to him and then being hurt when he leaves." *I don't want to be hurt when he leaves.* "You and Rosa should be careful, too. Daniel Trent will not last until to the new year. I promise."

Washing her hands a few minutes later, Willa met her own gaze in the mirror. *"I promise,"* she'd said.

"Hah," she told her reflection. "You *hope!*"

LATE THAT NIGHT, IN THE ROOM they'd shared since they were children, Lili put aside her book to look at her sister, seated at the dressing table brushing her hair. "Willa and Daniel had quite a confrontation this evening."

Rosa nodded. "And now she knows just how strong he really is."

"She's worried that he'll go after the rustlers on his own." Lili smoothed the covers over her knees. "Or with just his own men. One of them might get hurt."

"Nate Hernandez, for example?" Through the mirror, Rosa saw Lili's blush. "You haven't even gone up there to speak with him."

"Why would I?"

"So that he would know you're interested."

"I couldn't."

Rosa turned around. "Lili, that's always been the problem. You've never let Nate know, and so he thinks you don't care. Maybe by the time you both get to be eighty years old, you'll come to your senses about that."

"If he were truly interested, he'd come here."

"After Jamie accused him of stealing and fired him? What sort of man would he be if he came back under those circumstances?"

"Jamie's been gone for nearly two years."

"And Nate has his pride." With her hair braided, Rosa turned out the light on the dressing table and went to her own bed, identical to Lili's. "I suppose you can just sleep with me for the rest of our lives." Turning her back to her sister and the light, she said, "And we'll both die shriveled old maids."

The room plunged into darkness as Lili turned off the lamp by her bed. "You would be happier if I left you here by yourself?"

Touching the metal bracelet that never left her wrist, Rosa sighed. "I have my memories, Lilianna. They keep me company. I wish you could make some memories of your own, that's all. Before it's too late."

MONDAY MORNING, DANIEL WENT into Zapata to talk to the sheriff about the rustlers. Hobbs Sutton defied the stereotype of a fat, bumbling Texas sheriff, being tall and lean with black hair, sharp gray eyes and a ready smile.

"Good to meet you, Major Trent." He gave a firm, quick handshake. "Sorry I haven't made it out to your place yet."

"I imagine you stay pretty busy." Daniel lowered himself into the chair offered. "Law enforcement on the border is a challenge these days."

"You got that right." Sheriff Sutton sat down behind his paper-covered desk. "What can I do for you?"

"I understand there's been some cattle rustling in my part of the county—the northern side of the Blue Moon Ranch."

Sutton shook his head. "Yeah, Willa's lost a couple hundred head over the last few years." A flush spread over his cheekbones. "And I should have put a stop to it—don't think I don't know that. But I've got sixty miles of the Mexican border to patrol, plus the highways inside the county. I simply don't have the manpower to post a permanent watch on Willa's fence line. Or yours."

"I understand. Have other ranches been hit?"

The sheriff went into a drawer and pulled out a thick file folder. "These are reports of rustling just in this southeast area. And, yeah, quite a few resemble the evidence from Willa's place—time of day and month, probable number of suspects, use of a specific brand of ATV and cattle truck." He handed a sheaf of pages to Daniel. "I've clipped all those together. You're welcome to draw your own conclusions." When Daniel raised his eyebrows in surprise, Sutton grinned. "Since you're military, I figure we're basically working for the same boss."

In the end, Daniel had to admit the sheriff's department had done as much as could be expected. "These guys are too smart and too fast," he concluded. "Short of posting a full-time guard on the fences, I don't know what the answer is. I do know I can't afford to lose hundreds of cattle. My herd will be a tenth the size of Willa's."

Sutton got to his feet. "Amazing, isn't it? She's kept that place running since her husband left, practically single-handed. And managed three kids, in the process."

Daniel wondered if he heard a trace of personal interest in the sheriff's voice. "She's a determined woman. A little prickly, maybe."

"Well, she didn't want to sell off part of the land, you know. The Mercado legend carries a lot of weight around here, and Willa bought into it in a big way when she married Jamie. We all went to school together, first grade through high school."

"Maybe having a neighbor on her northern border will relieve her of some responsibility," Daniel said, though he'd scoffed at the idea in the confrontation with Willa. "I'll do what I can to catch these creeps."

"Don't put yourself at risk in the process. If you give me something concrete to work with, I'll bring in as many people as I can spare." He walked Daniel to his truck and shook his hand once more. "Be sure to tell Willa I'm ready for some of her aunts' home cooking, any time she issues an invitation!" Slapping a hand on the truck hood, Sutton gave a final wave and went back into the building.

So the sheriff was interested in Willa. Daniel picked up some groceries, then drove home wondering if Hobbs Sutton was the reason Willa was so upset about their night together. If she were dating Sutton but had let the alcohol sway her judgment…

Daniel shook his head. Not likely. A woman who could run a ranch the size of the Blue Moon without help wouldn't surrender to lust if her heart was given elsewhere. Sutton might intend to pursue Willa, but his reasoning told him she didn't intend to get caught.

What did that say about her feelings for Daniel, himself?

Driving across Blue Moon land toward his own house, he saw a small cloud of dust on the side of the road, which resolved, as he approached, into two kids with a brown-and-white dog. While Toby pulled on the leash attached to the dog's collar, Susannah attempted to propel the animal from behind with shooing motions and occasional shoves. But the dog—young, rawboned and playful—wiggled and plunged, going in every direction except the one Toby desired.

Daniel pulled up beside them and lowered his windows. "Is this obedience class?"

Toby came over to the truck and climbed up on the running board. "Hi, Major Trent. Boy, are we glad to see you."

Below window level, the dog echoed this sentiment with an excited bark…followed by the distinct sound of ten claws scraping down the finish on the door of Daniel's truck.

He cringed and Susannah gasped. "No, no, doggie. Get him down, Toby!" Judging by her face as she gazed at the door, a new paint job would be called for.

Toby disappeared, and then the passenger door opened. "Look what we got you," the boy said, levering the dog's hind end onto the seat. "Just what you need!"

Before Daniel could take a breath, the dog bounded into his lap. Wagging from the tip of his nose to the point of his tail, he proceeded to wash Daniel's face with his long, very wet tongue.

"Hey, hey. Stop. C'mon, dog. Stop!" Daniel got hold of the narrow shoulders and held the animal off. "Toby, where in the world did you get this animal?"

The dog lunged forward, trying to lick again. His face and one ear were caramel brown, and his short hair grew in brown and white splotches over his body and legs. All four paws, the remaining ear and the tip of his tail had stayed white.

"We found him on the road near the bus stop. Isn't he great?"

"Definitely a terrific dog." While the dog turned to look at

Toby, Daniel took a second to swipe a shirt sleeve across his face. "So terrific, in fact, that I really think you should keep him as your own." He got his hand back on the dog before the dog got in another lick.

"Mom won't let me bring any more animals home," Toby said, his lip stuck out in a pout. "Just because—"

"Just because the last time he brought home a pregnant gerbil…without telling her." His sister crinkled her nose in disgust. "We had gerbil babies running all over the house, 'cause he knocked over the box and couldn't get them back in."

Daniel had to grin. "That's pretty bad, Toby."

"Well, but the kid who brought her to school was going to drown her, because his mom wouldn't let him have anymore gerbils. Lucky is so pretty, I couldn't let her die like that."

"Lucky is still around?"

Susannah sighed. "She lives with a couple of her female babies in Toby's room. We made him take the rest to a pet store in Laredo."

"Lucky sounds like she lives up to her name. But I don't think—"

"No, really, Major Trent, you need a dog." Toby sat down in the passenger seat.

"Why?"

"To keep you company. To chase off coyotes. To warn you if somebody's coming."

The dog chose that moment to scratch furiously at his ear with a back foot, then turned and bit even more violently at the spot just above his tail.

"To bring fleas into my house," Daniel said, already resigned to the inevitable. He'd always had a soft spot in his heart for puppies, and this one did have an eager-to-please expression. "Have you named him?"

Toby smiled in triumph. "We wanted you to do that."

"Gee, thanks." Daniel pushed the dog into Toby's lap. "Put on your seat belt and hold him still until we get to the house. Hop in, Susannah. I guess I'm taking what's-his-name here home."

Once inside the house, the dog immediately peed on the vinyl floor of the kitchen.

"No, no." Toby took firm hold of the leash. "You do that outside. Outside." He pulled the dog through the kitchen door, across the carport and into the dirt, firmly repeating, "Outside."

"I'm so sorry." Susannah grabbed up the roll of paper towels on the counter. "I knew this wasn't a good idea, Major Trent. But I couldn't talk him out of it. And I couldn't let him come up here by himself. Mom doesn't know."

Daniel took the paper towels and did the cleanup himself. "Don't worry, Susannah. I don't mind having a dog. You're sure he doesn't belong to someone and just wandered off?"

"We've seen him for several days in a row. I think somebody dropped him off because they didn't want him anymore. And he kept waiting for them to come back." She knuckled tears out of her eyes. "I hate it when people do that."

"Me, too." He was completely hooked now, Daniel realized. "I just hope he's healthy."

Toby and the dog came through the door. "He did his business," the boy announced proudly. "See, he's practically house-trained already."

"Let's hope so." Daniel set a chair across the opening into the rest of the house. "Still, I think I'll keep him in the kitchen until I'm sure. Are you two hungry? I found a box of homemade cookies on my doorstep yesterday."

The three of them wolfed down a plate of Rosa Mercado's lemon cookies and a glass of milk each while the dog sniffed at every inch of the kitchen perimeter. Finally he flopped onto the rug in front of the sink. A minute later, he started to snore.

Daniel glared at Toby. "You brought me a dog who snores."

Toby winced. "Maybe he's got a little cold. Or allergies—it's hay fever season, isn't it?" When Daniel only shook his head in mock disgust, Toby said, "What will you call him?"

"Trouble."

"No, really."

"Really, that's his name." Daniel nodded. "The dog who scratched my truck door, got dirt all over my leather seats and peed on my kitchen floor…what else should I call him but Trouble?"

Toby considered. "Well, okay, then. Hey, Trouble." He went down on his knees beside the dog and rubbed his ears. "That's your name, boy. Do you like it? You're Trouble!" Wagging his tail, Trouble leapt to his feet and began scuffling playfully with his new friend. A minute later, he had vaulted the chair blocking the door and gone on to explore the rest of the house, with Toby in hot pursuit. "Trouble, come back. Trouble!"

Daniel looked at Susannah. "He's never heard the saying, 'Let sleeping dogs lie,' has he?"

She gave him her mother's bright smile. "I guess not."

Chapter Seven

With Trouble, Toby and Susannah once again in the truck, Daniel
drove down to the Mercado barn. The kids got out just as Willa,
inside the corral, took the saddle off a big red horse, which immediately bucked and jumped its way to the other side of the ring.

After setting the saddle on the top board of the fence, Willa
eased out of the corral gate. Hands propped on her hips, she
glanced at Daniel's truck, then surveyed her children. "Where
have you two been?"

Daniel had intended to get out, but he sat motionless, instead,
transfixed by the sight of Willa Mercado in a red tank top, snug
jeans, boots and leather chaps. The afternoon sun sheened the
well-shaped muscles in her arms and shoulders and chest, while
the low-riding chaps emphasized the feminine curve of her hips,
the slender length of her legs. The memory of their night together
surged over him—he relived the slide of her skin under his
palms, the softness of her breast against his lips, the heat of her
surrounding him. And his body reacted appropriately.

So he stayed in the truck while Toby ran to his mother, telling
the whole tale. As she listened, Willa's expression ran the
spectrum from irritated to impatient to embarrassed.

Sending Toby into the barn to start his chores, she came to
Daniel's window. "I'm sorry. If you want to take the dog to the

shelter, I'll explain it to him. You shouldn't let him impose on you like that." She glanced at Trouble, now sleeping in the passenger seat, and her mouth softened into a smile. "He is cute, isn't he?"

"He is. And I'm glad they didn't just leave him on the road to get hit. I've always wanted a dog, but I could never commit to a pet in the Army. He'll be good company."

Willa's gaze came back to his face. "Thanks for bringing them home. Again."

"No problem." Some devil inside him made him say, "I talked to Hobbs Sutton this morning. About the rustlers."

Though he watched closely, he didn't see a reaction that might signal romantic interest. She lifted one bare shoulder. "I'm sure he told you pretty much what I did. He doesn't have enough people to cover that area on a regular basis."

"He did say that. And I told him I'd see what I could do about catching the creeps. Who knows? Old Trouble might come in handy on that job."

Willa raised her eyebrows. Her eyes opened wide with concern. "You can't possibly take on a band of rustlers single-handed. Don't even try."

"Is that concern for my safety? Or doubt of my abilities?" Her hesitation made the point.

Daniel set his jaw. "My knee may be messed up, but I promise you, Willa, I can handle myself in a fight."

"Daniel—"

"Gotta go get dog food. Take care." Putting the window up between them, he shoved the gear stick into Reverse. As soon as Willa stepped back, Daniel swung the truck around and, with a spray of dust, left the woman who doubted him behind.

THANKS TO INFORMATION from Toby, Willa managed to be outside her barn when the trucks containing Daniel's cattle rumbled up the road. She knew the rancher who'd sold him the cows and would have bought some of the herd herself if she'd had the cash to spare. Daniel had gotten a fair deal on some very good animals, with help from Nate Hernandez.

She still couldn't believe Nate had left retirement to work for a ranch in competition with the Blue Moon. One of Jamie's biggest mistakes had been firing Nate, and she'd told him so at the time. But even after they'd discovered the missing tack—saddles and bridles worth several thousand dollars—in the possession of another ranch hand, Jamie had refused to apologize. Nate had a way of speaking his mind, and Jamie didn't handle criticism well.

Selfishly, she wondered whether Nate would come back to the Blue Moon when—if—Daniel left.

Those cattle trucks looked awfully permanent, though. Five of them passed through, each carrying twenty head of the longhorns Texas was famous for. Would Daniel, with Nate and three cowboys—more information from Toby—be able to get this many cows safely to pasture? Should she send some of her crew to help? Should she go herself?

Once the last truck disappeared, Willa knew she couldn't resist the urge to at least observe the arrival of Daniel's herd. With Monty already saddled for the day's work, all she had to do was enjoy a fast gallop across the fields, which brought her to a ridge overlooking Daniel's barn and the pens where he would unload the herd. She figured she'd stay unnoticed during the crazy work of unloading cattle and could slip away without anyone knowing she was there.

For all Daniel lacked experience in ranching, his setup looked good, probably thanks to Nate's advice. The chute fences appeared solid, and the hands stood where she would have placed them herself, as the first truck backed up to the gate. Daniel, she was glad to see, stood off to the side, out of the way of panicked cattle and the men who knew how to handle them. Of course, Nate would see to it that the boss stayed safe.

With the clang of the truck gate opening, controlled chaos began. Lowing and calling, the longhorns rushed toward freedom, down the long wooden chute toward the open ground of a holding pen beyond. At this time of year there were no babies with the bunch, but many of the cows were pregnant. Daniel would have his hands full come late winter and early spring.

Except he wouldn't be here for the calving, would he?

By lunchtime, all the cattle, including two prime-looking bulls, had been unloaded into the pens. Willa saw Daniel personally thank each driver before the empty trucks rattled back down the road. Standing at the top of the chute—now closed to prevent any cows from coming back up—he gave a sharp whistle.

"Lunch is served under the tent by the barn," he announced to his hands. "Come help yourselves." As the men started moving, Willa realized Daniel's gaze had focused on her across all the cattle between them. "That includes you, Willa," he shouted. "Please join us."

She couldn't very well refuse, not in front of his crew. Setting Monty into a jog, she rode around the pens and the milling cattle within until she reached the yard outside the barn, where Daniel himself waited for her.

"Your horse can join Calypso and the rest in the corral." He gave her the dignity of being able to dismount without help. "What did you think? Did we pass inspection?"

As she walked Monty to the corral, she felt her cheeks flush in embarrassment. She hadn't really come here to judge him…had she? "Everything went great, I thought. Looks like you've got some seasoned men on your crew. And Nate knows what he's doing, of course."

"Sure." Daniel moved with her toward the tent. He seemed to depend on the cane less than she remembered. "This afternoon the fun will start—getting them to the fields. I hope Calypso is ready for the ride."

She looked up at him in shock. "You're going to help move the cattle?"

He grinned. "I wouldn't be a rancher otherwise, would I?" He gestured to the stack of plates at the end of a long trestle table filled with food. "Help yourself."

"Thanks." As she moved down the line, Willa realized the food itself looked familiar. "Did you cook all of this?"

"Um…Miss Lili and Miss Rosa offered to help me out with some food for the guys while we were getting settled."

"I see." So if he wouldn't eat at the house, Lili and Rosa were going to bring him food. "They didn't mention it."

"They've been feeding me, too," he said, as if needing to get everything off his chest. "And sometimes I find boxes of cookies or cake on my front steps."

"And don't forget to mention that you had my older son working for you," Willa told him, as they faced each other across the barn aisle, sitting on bales of hay. "And my younger son and my daughter brought you a dog."

"And cats." Daniel jerked his head toward the loft above them. "Somewhere they found a nest of kittens and their mother, all of which are now cozily installed in a box up there."

Willa allowed her jaw to drop. "Why did you let them do that?"

He shrugged. "A barn does need cats. As long as Trouble gets along with them, we'll be fine."

Shaking her head, she dug her fork into Lili's chicken casserole. "Somebody is crazy here. I'm just not sure who."

ROSA KEPT AN EYE OUT as the New Moon hands came through the food line she and Lili had set up. Nate Hernandez shooed the rest of the men, as well as Daniel and Willa, ahead of him before picking up a paper plate for his own food. He took a long time choosing between chicken casserole and sliced ham, ending up with a good helping of both, then carefully selected his roll, a brownie and two chocolate chip cookies. As a result, everyone else had found a place to sit and eat by the time Nate reached Lili, waiting to pour him a drink.

"Good afternoon, Miss Lili." Somehow, he managed to hold his plate, his hat and a fork all in one hand.

"Good afternoon, Nate." She was blushing, of course, which made her cheeks rosy and her eyes bright. "What would you like to drink? We have sweet tea, lemonade, water and coffee."

"Is that your homemade lemonade? I don't think I've had anything quite as thirst-quenching in my life as your lemonade."

"We made it just this morning." Lili gave him a shy smile, and then it was Nate's turn to turn red in the face. "Here's a nice full glass." She held out the plastic cup.

Nate stared at the drink, as if he wasn't sure how to take hold of it. "Thank you." He closed his fingers around the drink and they both jumped.

Rosa smiled to herself. It was about time those two actually touched each other, even if it was only a couple of fingers.

The foreman cleared his throat. "Have you eaten, Miss Lili?"

"I—"

Rosa could see that her sister meant to divert what was obviously an invitation. "No, she hasn't." She handed Lili a plate. "Get yourself some food and sit down to eat. That's what I'm going to do. All the men are served and they can manage their own seconds." With a full plate of her own, she went to sit beside Luis Vargas, the youngest and most handsome of Daniel's cowboys. What was the point of being an old woman if she couldn't flirt with any young man who took her fancy?

Nate and Lili, she was pleased to see, sat hip to hip on one of the hay bales set under the tent, facing in opposite directions so they could see each other as they ate. Lili still seemed shy, and Nate didn't say much, but at least they'd made contact. Surely they could manage their own romance from this point without so much stage-managing from a concerned older sister.

Or not. Rosa watched, frustrated, as Nate stood, gave Lili a small bow, then dropped his trash into the bin and walked toward the back of the barn. Lili gazed after him with a wistful smile.

"Men," Rosa muttered, casting an angry glance at Luis.

The young man gave a puzzled shrug. "What'd I do?"

"You were born, to start with." Getting to her feet, she marched back to the food table to begin cleaning up. "It's all downhill from there."

AFTER LUNCH, THE HANDS gathered near their parked trucks to smoke before saddling up. "Nate takes a thirty-minute nap every afternoon," Daniel told Willa. "If that's what keeps him so fit at almost seventy, I'm going to start scheduling one into my day."

She stretched her arms out wide, full of good food and, for once, completely relaxed. "I can understand the appeal. I wouldn't mind lying down for a few minutes myself right now."

When she turned her head to smile at Daniel, she didn't find him smiling in response. The intensity, the *hunger,* in his face made her suddenly aware of how her T-shirt stretched thinly across her breasts, how the V-neck showed a little cleavage. She sat on a hay bale with her feet planted on the floor and her knees wide apart, which now seemed like an invitation…an invitation, Willa realized suddenly, she desperately wanted to give.

In the next moment, Daniel was on his feet, moving to dump his paper plate and drink can in the trash. "It's time to get started," he said over his shoulder. "You're welcome to stay and watch…or help, if you want. I'm sure we could use extra hands."

After that, he was all business as he reviewed with the

cowboys which pasture they would be driving the first herd to. Willa knew the land better than anyone there, even Nate—knew the gullies and ridges they would cross, the places where a cow might wander or stumble or spook. Listening to Daniel, she realized that he had studied the landscape and taken all those obstacles into account. Since he couldn't rely on the kind of familiarity her years working this land had created, he'd assessed the terrain with his own military expertise and had arrived at pretty much the same conclusions. Willa could only be impressed.

Mounted on her horse and moving toward the herd with the rest of the crew, Willa found herself riding beside Daniel. "You and Calypso seem to be getting along. Is he working all right for you?"

Daniel glanced in her direction but didn't meet her eyes. "He's a great horse. I'd have eaten dirt quite a few times by now if he weren't so careful. You did a terrific job training him."

"Thanks." Perversely, because he didn't want to look at her, she wanted to make him do just that. "That's a nice saddle you put on him. Where'd you get it?"

In the shadow of his hat brim, his cheeks reddened. "I... uh...won it. At a rodeo, when I was sixteen."

"You were riding rodeos when you were a teenager?"

He nodded. "When I was a little kid, about six years old, we visited my uncle—my mother's brother—on his ranch in Wyoming. He was this cool guy with a big booming laugh who smoked and drank and enjoyed every minute of his life on the range. We went a couple more times, as a family, and then I went out during the summers, when my mom would let me fly by myself. Once, on a dare from the other hands, I signed up for the saddle bronc event at the local rodeo. And I won, thanks to beginner's luck." He laughed. "I tried several more times and got thrown almost before we'd cleared the gate."

She wanted to ask more, but they'd come up beside the chute, where the cowboys were getting ready to release the cattle. The time for talking had passed.

With a warning shout, one of the men released the catch on the gate and let it swing wide. Moments later, a cow or two recognized the chance for escape and meandered into the wider field, followed by their herd mates. Soon enough, a long line of cattle stretched across the ground, and men on horseback moved into place, directing the flow with the angle and motion of their horses. They didn't have far to go, about two miles across country. As she eased Monty toward a cow that had veered away from the herd, Willa relaxed in her saddle. This was going to go just fine.

And then Trouble came streaking toward the herd, barking at the top of his canine lungs.

The smoothly moving line broke into clumps of startled cows, each clump moving in a different direction. Cowboys and horses reacted quickly, but there weren't enough of them to manage the breakdown. Longhorns were hard to spook, but as Trouble raced along, the cattle turned away from the barking dog, maybe seeking refuge in the pen behind them, maybe moving by blind instinct. A few of the lead cows picked up speed, starting to run. More and more of the herd joined them. In the next instant, they had a full-fledged longhorn stampede on their hands.

Willa didn't realize, until too late, that Daniel and Calypso stood directly in the path of the thundering herd.

Both man and horse froze for an instant. Willa held her breath, trying to see through the dust cloud thrown up by hundreds of pounding hooves, praying that Calypso would be fast enough, that Daniel could hang on through the chaos. For an instant, she saw them through the dust—saw Calypso at the near edge of the herd, ready to jump clear.

But then she saw Daniel throw up his hands, saw the reins fly free. In the next moment, both Calypso and Daniel disappeared underneath the roaring river of cattle.

HE'D BEEN HERE BEFORE, THIS PLACE where pain burned like the desert sun, relentless, inescapable. This time, at least, he could move, thrashing his arms and legs in a weak attempt to find some shade…

"Daniel. Daniel, relax." A cool hand caught one wrist, while another soothed his forehead. "You're okay. Just relax."

He peeked through a half-lifted eyelid, saw the pale walls of a hospital and groaned. "Not again."

"Open your eyes, Daniel." The same voice, husky, feminine, appealing. *Willa?* He did as instructed. "It's you."

"Welcome back, cowboy." She smiled at him but removed her hands, which made him wish he'd disobeyed her order. "That was quite a ride you took."

Daniel thought back and remembered. "Is Calypso okay? He tripped—I didn't see what was there—"

"An appropriately named dog was there."

"Trouble? How did he get out? I know I left him locked in the house. Is that dog some kind of Houdini?"

"He might be, given how many hooves he managed to dodge in the process of causing a stampede." Willa shook her head. "How the three of you survived intact is something I'll never understand."

A sudden stab of pain through his temple left Daniel wincing. "Intact might be an overstatement."

"You've been out for a couple of hours. You probably do have a headache."

He made an exploratory move of his arms and legs. "Plus some bruises."

"But no broken bones," a third voice informed him, as a woman wearing green surgical scrubs strode into the room. "And no damage to that erector set of pins and shafts holding your right leg together." She offered Daniel a handshake. "I'm Dr. Dobbins. Other than the concussion, you're in good shape.

We'll let you stay overnight, just to keep an eye on you, then send you home in the morning."

Before he could protest, she gave a quick wave and hurried off. Daniel frowned at Willa, instead. "I don't need to stay overnight."

She laughed at him. "I would have predicted you'd say that. Men never want to follow medical advice. But I can tell you that I'm not taking you home, and there's nobody else here to do it. So unless you're planning to walk, I'd say your best bet is to do as you're told."

"I've taken more medical orders than any one person ought to put up with," he grumbled, even though he knew the cause was lost. "I thought I was finished with hospitals."

"Occupational hazard. Most folks who work with cattle and horses have to visit them now and again." Leaning back in her chair, she glanced at their bland surroundings. "At least you got as far as the hospital. Jamie didn't."

Daniel sensed she didn't want an apology. "How long was he in the National Guard?"

"He joined at the start of the war. He had a lot to say about patriotism and defending the country, but I think he was looking for excitement. Contrary to today's experience, ranch life gets to be pretty routine after a while."

"He had to know the risks, though."

She shrugged. "Jamie liked taking risks, with money and with his own safety. Toby's just like him—reckless, adventurous, usually forgets to look before he leaps. Robbie and Susannah are more like me, thank goodness."

"Cautious," Daniel suggested. "Always prepared."

"I prefer knowing what to expect."

"Is that why you married a man you'd known all your life?"

Willa gasped and jumped to her feet. "What gives you the right to ask that kind of question?"

"Blame it on the concussion. Are you going to answer?"

She stalked to the window and looked out, keeping her back to him. "It's none of your business."

"I disagree." He waited through a long silence, wondering if she would trust him enough to explain.

Finally, her shoulders lifted and sank again. "My sophomore year in high school, I fell madly in love with the captain of the football team."

"Jamie?"

The long braid hanging down her back swayed as she shook her head. "On our first date, he told me he loved me. After a week, he told me if I loved him, I'd go all the way. So I did."

Daniel winced.

"By the next school day," she continued, "the whole football team knew what I'd done, and they made sure to tell everyone else. Teachers looked at me differently, thinking I was a slut. My mother found out, though somehow my dad never did. Or didn't care enough to say anything."

Finally, she turned around and gazed at him, her face expressionless. "Jamie had been my friend since first grade. He knew it was my first time, and he knew how upset I was when Mr. Football never called again. We hung out together and gradually fell in love. That's why I married him."

"I understand." He searched for the right words. "Willa, I'm not the evil Mr. Football."

"I know. And there are lots of reasons I should fall into your arms, begging you to be part of my life." She stuck up her thumb. "You're great with my kids. My aunts love you." Her index finger came up. "You've obviously got a decent amount of money." Middle finger. "You're a sincerely nice man—" ring finger "—and you're terrific in bed." All five slender fingers stretched long.

Daniel grinned. Willa did not, but she stuck up her other thumb. "I admit I could use your help and your support."

Dropping her arms, she braced her hands on the footboard of his bed. "But I simply don't want to take the risk."

"There's no risk, Willa." He stretched his arms out wide. "I am what you see."

Her smile was rueful as she shook her head. "There's always a risk. Jamie should have been the safest choice of all, and look what happened." She sighed. "These days, what I want is to take care of my family and the Blue Moon. It's enough."

"You deserve more, Willa. I'd like to give you more."

"That's sweet." She gave him a small, sad smile. "But as your friend, I'm telling you not to waste your time."

A nurse poked her head through the open doorway. "Visiting hours are ending. You'll need to leave."

Willa straightened her back. "Right." Her gaze, when she looked at Daniel, was distant. "Nate said he would be here tomorrow morning to take you home. I hope you get some sleep tonight."

"Willa—" He stretched out a hand.

But she shook her head, turned and quickly left the room.

Daniel let his arm drop to the bed. Exhaustion overpowered him suddenly, and he sank back against the pillow, letting his eyes close. His first day as a full-fledged rancher had ended in disaster. What did that say about his chances for long-term success? He had a feeling the odds against him had gone up significantly.

If Willa wasn't part of the package, though, maybe he didn't care.

Chapter Eight

Willa drove home with the radio tuned to one of the kids' rock stations and turned up loud, hoping the unfamiliar music would keep her from thinking about…well, anything, really. Over dinner, she gave the favorable report on Daniel's condition to Lili and Rosa and the children, then escaped as soon as possible, pleading paperwork to finish.

What greeted her on her desk, of course, was the October calendar, its first days marked off with big red X's. She gazed at the blank days still to come, thinking about her conversation with Daniel at the hospital. Seventy-four days until December twenty-first. Would she hold out against him that long? Would he take her at her word and stop trying?

What would she do if he didn't leave by Christmas?

Avoiding the questions she couldn't answer, Willa turned her attention to paying bills and figuring accounts. Unfortunately, the picture presented by those accounts and the remaining balance in her checkbook was a grim one, indeed. Daniel's payment had only postponed the crisis. If she couldn't figure out more ways to economize, she'd have to cut back on her crew, all of whom needed their jobs. Last summer's sales had covered the costs of production, with nothing left over for expansion or decreasing her debt. She could sell part of the herd—at the wrong time of year, with prices down. Her profit lay in marketing fat calves, not pregnant heifers. But if she changed her tax structure…

When the numbers didn't look any better at midnight than they had at 10:00 p.m., she forced herself to quit calculating and go to bed. On the way to her room, however, the clatter of pans drew Willa toward the kitchen. From the doorway, she saw Susannah working busily at the counter, reading a recipe book at the same time as she stirred something dark and chocolatey in one of Rosa's big mixing bowls.

"What's the occasion?" Willa asked. "Did I miss the announcement of a bake sale?"

Susannah jumped and dropped her spoon into the bowl. "Mom!" Her voice squeaked in surprise and, Willa thought, embarrassment. "What are you doing up?"

"What are *you* doing still awake this late on a school night?"

"Um…well, I forgot to tell anybody about the bake sale." Her daughter wiped a hand across her face, leaving smears of chocolate on her smooth skin. "So I figured I'd better take care of it myself."

Willa crossed to the counter. "What are you making?" She turned the recipe book in her direction. "Chocolate fudge cake with black cherry frosting? Sounds pretty decadent for a school bake sale."

Susannah shrugged. "I wanted something different. Everybody makes brownies."

"That's true." Willa scooped up a fingerful of batter. "Mmm. Shall I stay and help?"

"No!" Susannah shook her head firmly. "I'm doing this all by myself. You should go on to bed." She gazed at Willa with a softer expression. "You look tired, Mom. You work too hard."

"Hard work is good for you." She said it automatically, because that's what mothers were supposed to tell their children.

"You always say that." Susannah butted her hip against Willa's, pushing her away from the counter. "Go on. I can do this all by myself."

Lying in bed, in the dark, Willa willed herself to sleep, without success. Her body refused to relax, and her mind wouldn't slow down. She did work hard, all day, every day. She hadn't had a vacation since Jamie was killed, and for several years before. He'd spent the money on some wild scheme or the other. There'd never been a good time to get away.

You deserve more, Willa. I'd like to give you more.

I simply don't want to take the risk.

But in her dreams that night, she wished she could.

WHEN DANIEL AND NATE PARKED in the carport Tuesday morning, they found a small cardboard box on the kitchen doorstep. Feeling every bruise he'd acquired in yesterday's fall, Daniel picked up the box and carried it inside to the table. After a long welcome session with Trouble—who looked none the worse for having challenged fifty longhorn cows the day before—they prepared to unveil the latest treat from the Mercado kitchen.

"A cake," Nate guessed. "No doubt Miss Rosa and Miss Lili wanted to welcome you home."

"Cookies would be good, too." Daniel removed the box's lid. "Nope, you win. It's…" He hesitated, gazing at the concoction he'd revealed. "I think it's a cake."

"It's round, anyway. The top's kinda bumpy."

"And slanted. That bulge around the middle indicates two layers, doesn't it?"

"I hope so. Or else it's gonna erupt."

"What flavor do you think the pink icing is?"

"Uh…strawberry?"

"Maybe. Get a knife and we'll see what the inside looks like."

The interior of the cake was a gooey chocolate. "Strawberry and chocolate." Nate scratched his head. "I'll eat a piece if you will."

Daniel took a deep breath. "Sure. Why not?"

Armed with plates and forks, they each took a helping. "Tastes better than it looks," was Nate's conclusion.

"That wouldn't be too hard." Daniel dragged his fork through the half-baked cake. "I have to say, this isn't up to the Mercado ladies' usual standard."

"No, it ain't. Maybe they weren't feeling too good."

"I don't think I'd be feeling too good if I ate any more of this…cake." With Trouble hopefully observing, he scraped his plate into the trash, did the same for Nate's and dropped the box with the remainder into the can. "So, are we driving more cattle this afternoon?"

After Daniel's fall, Nate and the hands had needed the rest of the day to round up the scattered cattle and convey them to their proper place. Today, with Trouble locked in his crate inside the locked house, they moved another group of cows to pasture before dark.

"Half-done," Daniel commented as they unsaddled back at the barn that afternoon.

"We should get the rest settled by dark tomorrow." Nate rubbed a rag over Daze's chest, back and belly.

Daniel used a brush on Calypso's white-and-black coat. "I wonder how long it'll take the rustlers to move in."

Nate said, "Not long enough."

But Daniel hoped that, for once, his foreman would be wrong.

WILLA'S CREW KNEW BETTER than to interrupt when she was breaking in a horse. So when Jorge hailed her to take a phone call in the middle of a ride on Wednesday morning, she knew immediately that a problem had come up.

Still, she wasn't prepared for the principal's voice. "Mrs. Mercado, I need you to come to school right away."

She gripped the phone tightly. "Are the kids all right?"

"Everyone is fine. But I have Robbie in my office, and I must see you as soon as possible."

Thirty minutes later, Willa strode into the school building and struggled against a tide of children to reach the administrative suite.

Her breathing eased a little when she saw Robbie sitting safe and sound in front of the principal's desk. But the sullen look on his face and the rigid set of Mrs. Abrams's shoulders signaled trouble.

"What is it?" she asked, still standing. "What has he done?"

Mrs. Abrams took a deep breath. "He brought this to school." With an unsteady hand, she indicated the big, black weapon lying in the center of her desk.

"A gun?" Willa swung around to stare at her son. "You brought a gun to school?"

"Is this yours, Mrs. Mercado?"

"No!" Willa didn't take her eyes off Robbie. "Why would you do something so…so stupid?"

Robbie shrugged one shoulder and lowered his gaze to the floor between his shoes. Taking one stride, Willa grabbed his shoulder and jerked.

"You will sit up like a man when you're in the principal's office, do you hear me?" Her voice shook with the effort not to scream. "And I want an answer. Why did you bring a weapon to school?"

Her son straightened up in the chair. "I thought it was cool. I thought the guys would like to see it."

"Where did the gun come from?" Mrs. Abrams came around to stand beside Willa. "Did someone give it to you?"

When Robbie didn't answer, Willa tightened her grip and

shook his shoulder again. "Answer the question, Roberto. Who gave you the gun?"

He flinched away from her. "Nobody!"

"You took it? Without permission?"

His silence confirmed her guess. Willa released him and faced the principal. "I know whose weapon this is. My neighbor is retired Army. He is not a danger to the school or the community in any way. Roberto must have…" God, it was hard to say! "…must have stolen the weapon from this man to bring to school."

The principal nodded. "I see." Returning to her chair, she sat down and propped her forearms on the desk. "Well, Mrs. Mercado, I'm sure you realize what a serious offense this is. We have zero tolerance for weapons of any kind at this school."

"I know." Willa sank into the chair beside Robbie's. "My son does, as well."

"The punishment for bringing a gun to school is automatic suspension. I'm allowed some latitude in determining the duration, but the minimum, as directed by the school board, is four weeks. All academic work during that period will receive a failing grade."

With her hands gripped together, Willa held onto her control. "I understand."

Mrs. Abrams smiled slightly. "Robbie's always been a good student, and we've never before had the slightest trouble with him. I believe this incident is unique and will not happen again. So I'm going to impose the minimum suspension."

Aware of the irony, Willa said, "Thank you."

"There will, of course, be a report to the sheriff's office, and I expect they will want to interview Robbie. If the local media gets hold of the story…" She shrugged her shoulders. "I'm sorry."

"No, I'm sorry." Willa got to her feet. A single glance at her son brought him out of his chair. He stood for a moment without speaking but then saw the second, furious look Willa sent in his direction.

"I'm sorry, too, Mrs. Abrams." Hands in his pockets, shoulders slumped, he managed to look the principal in the eye. "I didn't plan to hurt anybody. I didn't bring the bullets. I just—" He shrugged, then sniffed. When he turned his face away, Willa knew he was crying.

Well, she would be, too, when she had the privacy. "Thank you for your tolerance."

"I'll be in touch." Mrs. Abrams ushered them to the door. "And I will look forward to having Robbie back in school."

"He'll be a changed boy," Willa said. "I can promise you that."

The walk outside through the lunchtime rush might have been as much punishment as Robbie needed—silence fell as the crowd of kids parted to let them through, with all eyes focused on the boy who'd so completely screwed up. Willa didn't shield him or say a word, hoping the ostracism would do some good.

Once in the truck and on the way home, she waited for some kind of voluntary statement from her son. Finally, though, she gave in and broke the silence herself. "Talk to me, Roberto."

For another five miles, he resisted. "I just wanted to show the guys," he said, at last.

"Show them Major Trent's weapon? Why?"

Robbie shook his head. "Not him, so much. I figured... figured Dad would have used one like that. But Trent told me what it was like, being a soldier, fighting the war. I thought the gun would show how cool it was."

Now Willa was the one who let the silence lengthen. "Have you been...hassled...about your dad?"

His one-shouldered shrug meant yes.

"But, son, you had to know how much trouble you'd be in if

anyone found out about the gun. How many news reports have we seen about kids who brought weapons to school and what happens to them?" Then, when he didn't reply, she supplied the response herself. "You thought it was worth the risk."

There didn't seem to be much more to say. When they reached the house, Willa unlocked the doors and looked at Robbie. "Go to your room and stay there until I get back. You're grounded from the TV, telephone and video games. Understand?"

He nodded and left the truck without looking at her. Willa made sure he went inside, then followed to be sure Lili and Rosa understood the program. "He can eat lunch in his room," she told them. "I'll be back within the hour."

Lili pursued her to the front door. "Where are you going?"

Willa climbed into her truck and slammed the door. "To give someone a piece of my mind."

She found Nate Hernandez working in Daniel's barn and learned that "the boss" was in the house. Her knock on the front door was answered by Trouble's frantic bark. In the moments before the door opened, she noticed the landscaping Daniel had added to the place—lantana bushes along the front of the house, young pecan trees planted at intervals and mulched with bark to preserve moisture, plus a gravel walk curving from the front step to the driveway. The plain concrete block house was beginning to look like…a home.

The door swung back and Daniel stood there in jeans, a chambray shirt and bare feet. "Hey, Willa. Come on in."

She steeled her heart against that knee-weakening grin and stepped past him into the living room. "Do you have a few minutes?"

"Sure." He closed the door. "Let me release Trouble—he won't stop barking until he sees who's here." He went through to the kitchen. "Yes, she came just to see you," Willa heard him tell the dog. "Doesn't say much for her taste in men, I'll tell you that."

Trouble rushed in, wagging furiously from nose to tail and sniffing at her boots. Willa gave him a minute of attention, then straightened up to look at Daniel.

"Have a seat." He gestured to the big black leather recliner, and prepared to seat himself on a displaced kitchen chair.

"No, thanks."

Halfway to sitting, he struggled back to his full height. "What's wrong?"

"That's what I said, about two hours ago, when the principal of Robbie's school called."

"Something happened? Is he okay?"

"Oh, sure, he's great—except for being suspended for an entire month of classes, with failing grades for every assignment and test."

"Why?"

"Because, Major Trent, my son decided to win friends and influence people by taking your damn gun to school with him."

Daniel just stared at her for a minute. "My gun? Are you sure?"

"That's what he said."

His gaze turned inward, and then he left the room without a word. Willa followed him to the bedroom, where he stood with his hands on his hips, gazing at a moving box in the far corner. The tape on the top had been pulled up, then pressed into place again to disguise the fact that the box had been tampered with.

"The weapon was in here," he said. "I hadn't opened the box yet. I've ordered a gun safe, but the shipper appears to be having trouble finding Zapata, Texas."

She couldn't keep from glancing around Daniel's bedroom. Between the iron headboard and footboard, his bed was neatly made up, with crisp white sheets and a dark blue blanket. A gorgeous Turkish carpet covered the floor with a blue and cream and orange pattern. The only other furnishings were an armchair in a small orange check, a chest of drawers in dark wood with iron knobs and a lamp table by the bed…a simple, uncluttered space, like the man, himself.

"I drove the box across country in my truck," he continued. "But I did ask Rob to help me move it into this room." His chin dropped to his chest. "I suppose we know how Trouble got loose. Rob came in during the cattle drive to take the gun, and he let the dog out."

Willa fought the urge to apologize. "Probably. But the idea would never have occurred to him if you hadn't shown him the weapon and brainwashed him about the glory of being a soldier."

Daniel jerked around to face her. "I don't know what you're talking about."

"Telling him stories about war, Daniel. Feeding his desperate need to resurrect his father, by telling him just what he wanted to hear—tales of your adventures in the desert, the brotherhood of combat, the excitement of taking out the enemy."

"I didn't—"

"You made yourself and Jamie heroes in Robbie's eyes, and he couldn't wait to share with his friends at school. He took the gun with him to back up what he was saying."

"This is not my fault, Willa. I did not show him the weapon. I told him the box contained uniforms, boots and junk. He must have guessed the truth."

"You're saying he lied to me."

"I'm afraid he did."

"Are you denying you told him about the war?"

"N-no. He asked, and I did answer his questions."

"In the process, encouraging him to think about his father's exploits as some kind of…of knightly crusade."

"I did no such thing. And I refuse to apologize for serving my country, or for being damn good at it."

"I'm not asking you to. But you didn't have to make it look

so desirable." She pressed her clenched fist against her mouth. "I lost my husband to the military. I will not give up my sons, as well."

"That's a long way in the future, Willa. By then your boys will have the right to make their own decisions."

"I will never accept their right to take that kind of risk with their lives."

Daniel watched as Willa pulled herself together. He wanted to put his arms around her, assure her that she could handle whatever happened. But that was another kind of risk she wasn't prepared to accept.

He followed when she turned and, without a word, returned to the living room. "What are you going to do about Robbie?"

She stopped with her hand on the front doorknob. "Work his butt off, so he'll understand why staying in school is a good thing."

"Do I get a say in this?" Now she looked at him, with anger and indignation on her face. Daniel held up a hand. "Two points. First, Robbie stole from me. I'm an injured party, here."

Some of the outrage faded. "I guess that's true."

"More important, though… You say this is my fault. Shouldn't I have some role in setting Rob straight again?"

Relief flashed in her eyes. "What would you do with him?"

Daniel grinned. "Work his butt off."

THAT AFTERNOON, A HEAVY KNOCK on Daniel's door announced the arrival of Sheriff Hobbs Sutton. "I have something that belongs to you," he said, holding up the gun inside a clear plastic bag. "You have some paperwork?"

"Come on in, Sheriff." He'd anticipated this visit and had all his permits ready to show. "Would you like a cup of coffee? It's a little cool out there today."

"Sounds good." Sutton set the gun down on the kitchen table

and paged through the notebook in which Daniel kept his records. "You've got quite an arsenal here."

"Occupational hazard," Daniel said, borrowing the phrase from Willa. He gave the sheriff a mug of coffee. "I have a safe coming and will guarantee that no one but me ever opens it."

"All right. There are plenty of kids with guns in this county already, crossing back and forth across the border, generally raising hell. I don't need any more of 'em, especially not with the kinds of weapons you've got here."

"Will there be charges against Rob?"

Sutton shook his head. "I believe his story—he wanted to show off. What thirteen-year-old doesn't? Unless…" He cocked an eyebrow at Daniel. "Unless you want to press charges for theft."

"Nope. I'm devising my own brand of hard time."

"That's what the boy needs. That, and a daddy." Sutton stared into his coffee for a second. "Not gonna happen any time soon, though." He blew out a deep breath, then drained the mug in three gulps. "Gotta go. Seen any sign of those rustlers yet?"

"Not yet. We check the perimeter daily." As they stepped outside, a gust of chilly air swept across the yard. "Maybe they've relocated to a warmer climate."

"Maybe." Sutton climbed into his truck. "Good luck with your inmate. Temper your justice with mercy, as they say."

BUT ROB'S ATTITUDE, at 8:00 a.m. on Monday morning, did nothing to elicit mercy, or even concessions. Willa pulled up next to Daniel's barn, waved without smiling as Rob left the truck, then drove off. Looking ashamed, defiant and a little scared, the boy stood in front of Daniel and Nate with his hands in his back pockets. He didn't volunteer an apology, didn't say a word.

Daniel simply stared at him for a long moment. "Fine. I didn't want to talk this morning, anyway. You can start by stripping the stalls down to the dirt. I expect a new load of shavings about ten o'clock, so you should be finished by then."

Rob's eyes widened—it was a big job for two hours. Then he caught his breath and went into the barn.

The rest of the week followed the pattern of that first day. No conversation with Rob, no sharing jokes or stories, no praise for a job well done—just unremitting hard work. Daniel and Nate between them found some of the dirtiest, sweatiest tasks on the ranch and gave them to Rob. After the cold snap over the weekend, the weather turned warm again, and everybody complained about the ninety-degree temperatures. Everybody except Rob. The boy didn't say a word. His mother waved from behind the wheel of her truck but never lowered the window or got out to speak.

Daniel thought it was probably the worst week of his life since he'd awakened up in a hospital in Germany with his leg shattered and his Army career finished. The only bright spots were the boxes of treats that kept showing up on his doorstep. Chocolate chip cookies on Tuesday, brownies on Wednesday and an apple pie on Thursday, each steadily improving in quality over that first sad cake. Between them, Daniel, Nate and the hands finished every crumb.

Friday morning, while Rob swept five or six years' worth of cobwebs out of the barn, Daniel drove to Zapata to pick up mail from his post office box. Among the bills and the advertisements was a thick, cream-colored envelope, the kind invitations arrived in. Daniel dumped the rest of the mail on the passenger seat and opened the foil-lined envelope to see who wanted him and where.

The South Texas Cattlemen's Association
cordially invites you to the annual
Halloween Costume Ball
Saturday, October 19th, 8 p.m. until…

This year's theme is Texas History Night
Come dressed as your favorite character
from our Great State's past!

Twenty-four hours didn't give him much time to work up a costume. And the response date was two weeks ago, although Daniel doubted they'd refuse to take his money if he offered to buy a ticket. Only one factor would determine whether he stayed home tomorrow night watching a movie on TV or dressed up and headed out to dance the night away in a hotel in Laredo.

Would Willa Mercado be there?

Chapter Nine

"Who is that gorgeous man?"

Willa had been at the ball for an hour, dancing with Hobbs Sutton and Juan Angelo, drinking her first glass of champagne and catching up with friends, like Bev Drummond, who'd asked the question.

"What man?" Willa glanced around the ballroom at a motley collection of Sam Houstons, Davy Crocketts, Mexican generals and Spanish explorers, oil tycoons and Texas Rangers. "Where?"

"In the doorway." Bev, dressed as a nineteenth century "fallen angel," nodded her ostrich-plume headdress toward the entrance, but the crowd on the dance floor blocked Willa's view. "He's the winner of the costume contest, hands down. And we should auction him off as the most eligible bachelor of the night... assuming he is. Please, God, let him be single."

"I don't... Oh." The band finished its first set and the dancers dispersed, leaving her a straight line of sight to the man in the doorway. "Yes, he's single. That's—that's my new neighbor. Daniel Trent."

Bev grabbed her arm. "You know him? Introduce us, Willa. Please. And then leave quickly."

Willa laughed, as she was meant to, but she couldn't take her eyes off Daniel. He'd chosen a simple, yet perfect, costume—

white, long-sleeved shirt with a red bandanna at the throat, indigo blue jeans, leather chaps and a well-worn pair of boots. One hand held a white Stetson hat at his side. He embodied everyone's hero, the quintessential Texas cowboy, dressed up for a local barn dance.

Not every cowboy could boast those deep blue eyes, of course, or the wide shoulders and narrow waist. And only Daniel offered that sweet, sexy grin over which Bev was drooling.

"Come on." The redhead started across the floor, pulling Willa with her. "I want to meet this man. I want to dance with him. I want to bear his children."

Willa hung back, her stomach twisting in a disagreeable way at the thought of Bev with Daniel *that way*. But her friend simply jerked her closer, bearing down on her target with fierce determination.

Daniel's smile widened as Willa met his gaze. And then she was standing in front of him, with Bev simmering beside her.

"Hi," Willa said lamely. "It's, um, good to see you."

"You, too." He gave her a quick wink, then looked at Bev. "I'm Daniel Trent, Willa's new neighbor."

"This is Beverly Drummond," Willa said. "She owns Drummond's Feed Store in Zapata and is something of a local legend—a prize-winning barrel racer and winner of the Miss Texas Rodeo title. Bev, this is Daniel."

Bev extended her hand and Daniel took it. "I'm not surprised you're a pageant winner. A business woman and an athlete, as well? That's impressive."

Talkative Bev was practically speechless. "You're too good to be true."

"Oh, no, I'm not." He released her hand and looked at Willa again. "I understand Susannah's successful at barrel racing."

"Yes, indeed. Bev's been coaching her for several years now."

"She's competing next weekend in the Zapata County

Rodeo," Bev said. "I think Susannah's got a chance to beat the britches off every rider there. She and her pony are the best I've seen for quite some time."

"I might just have to show up and cheer for her."

Bev preened, as if he'd made the decision on her account. And for all Willa knew, he had. "We'll look forward to seeing you there." She put her hand to her ear, as if trying to hear the tune the band had just started up. "That sounds like a nice, cozy number. Will you dance with me, Daniel?"

He gave her a smile that would melt any woman's defenses. "How about the next slow one? Willa promised me the first dance after I got here."

Willa caught her jaw just before it dropped open in surprise.

"No fair, girlfriend." Bev's pout was only half teasing. "You're not supposed to steal the good ones before the rest of us get a chance." She fluttered her fingers at Daniel. "I'll be back," she promised, and drifted away.

"Are you impressed with my finesse?" Daniel put a hand on Willa's back and eased her toward the dance floor. "Not only did I manage to send her on her way smiling, but I made it impossible for you to refuse to dance with me." His arms slipped around her and the next thing she knew, they were swaying to a soft, dreamy tune.

"You can dance," Willa said, her voice weak. The last time they were this close… The memory took her breath away.

"Slowly," Daniel agreed. "And nothing too fancy."

She drew back a little to look at him. "You don't have your cane tonight?"

"I didn't think it went with the costume." He pulled her close again. "Between climbing onto a horse several times a day and working outside from dawn until dusk, my leg's holding up better than it used to. As long as I don't try to rush, I do okay." With his lips against her temple, he said, "You look beautiful."

"Th-thank you."

"Where did the dress come from?"

She'd been wondering if he'd noticed her costume. "Jamie's great-grandmother and her sisters embroidered the flowers and sewed the beads on the skirt and blouse. His grandmother and mother wore it for fiestas with the Mercado family in Mexico."

"And Susannah will wear it after you."

"I hope so."

"The family has quite a tradition to be proud of."

Again she pulled back to search his face. He wasn't making fun of the Mercados or her. "Yes, we do."

The music slowed, then stopped for a second before slamming into a hip-twisting rock number. Daniel winced. "I think I'll pass on this one." He glanced around as they left the floor. "If you'd like to find another partner…"

Willa shook her head. "Not really."

He grinned, and she had a chance to see that the expression started in his eyes with a glint of pleasure before the corners of his mouth lifted, and then the center. Totally devastating.

"We could get something to eat," she suggested. "And a glass of champagne."

"And hide from your friend."

Willa laughed. "And hide from Bev."

ROSA SAW DANIEL ENTER THE ballroom, and read the pleasure on his face when he glimpsed Willa through the crowd. Yes, indeed, that situation was developing quite nicely.

She'd wanted to mention the Cattleman's Ball to Daniel as soon as the invitations arrived. He should have come with them as Willa's escort. Her sister had convinced her to stand back, however, and let the two manage for themselves. Rosa had worried that Daniel simply wouldn't bother, but Lilianna had been right. That young man knew who he wanted and was prepared to go after her.

Which was more than could be said for Nate Hernandez.

Without telling Lili, Rosa had arranged to have the foreman sent an invitation to the ball. When Daniel had called to see if Willa would attend, Rosa had asked about Nate. Daniel had been sure that Nate had no intention of making an appearance. He didn't belong with the bigwigs, Daniel said, imitating Nate's drawl. That fancy shindig wasn't the place for plain ol' cowpokes like him.

Which was the problem, Rosa thought, watching Lili talk with the wives of some of the wealthiest and most influential cattle ranchers in the state. The Mercados boasted an old name, came from old money. If Texas had an aristocracy, they were part of it. And Nate simply wasn't.

But he'd loved Lili for years, since he'd come to the Blue Moon as a thirty-year-old drifter. And Lili loved him. Isolated on the ranch, sequestered by their father's old-fashioned ideas about a woman's place in the world, Rosa and Lili had missed most of life's adventures. Rosa's one rebellion had ended in tragedy. Lili had taken that lesson to heart and never reached for anything more.

Nate Hernandez was her last chance, and Rosa was determined to see her sister's hopeless dream come true. But she wasn't a fairy godmother and she didn't have a magic wand. Somehow she would have to get the two of them, Nate and Lili, to cooperate in their own happy ending. Or else they really didn't deserve one.

CARRYING PLATES AND GLASSES, Willa and Daniel found an empty bench in the lobby outside the ballroom. He gave a low groan as he sat down.

Willa frowned at him. "Maybe you should have brought the cane, after all."

He shifted his hips, easing the stiff leg, and gave her a rueful glance. "Maybe."

"Even cowboys get hurt now and then."

"I noticed. Eat your cream puff."

Willa realized she hadn't been this hungry in days. Weeks, maybe. She didn't stop until her plate was empty. "They always have great food at this party."

"I'm glad you came. Rosa told me you almost stayed home."

"You talked to her about it?"

"Well, there wasn't much point in being here if you weren't."

She gazed at him, speechless once again.

He clinked his champagne glass against hers. "So, I've heard a good deal about the Mercado legacy, one way or another. What about your family? Did you grow up on a ranch?"

"Yes. Yes, I did." She looked down at her own glass, then took a long sip. "We had a small place not too far from the Blue Moon."

"Did you raise cattle? Horses? Rattlesnakes?"

She gave an unwilling laugh. "Cattle. And rattlers. I must've killed hundreds before I got out of high school."

"That makes you a good shot."

"Yes, it does."

When she didn't volunteer anything else, he said, "Do your parents still live on that ranch?"

"Um…no. They sold off the land and moved away. We…" She took a deep breath. "We don't see them much."

"Do you have brothers and sisters?"

"I was the only child."

"Me, too. My parents were in their forties when I was born. I was a surprise, to say the least."

"A good one, I hope."

"Yeah, we were close. They died within a couple of months of each other six years ago."

"I'm sorry."

"Thanks. So where did your parents move to?"

Here was the question, and answer, she dreaded. "My mother

moved to Florida. My dad went to California." After a pause, she finished the explanation. "They had to get married, because she was pregnant. They stayed married only because of me. As soon as I got engaged to Jamie, even before the wedding, they divorced. As far as I know, they haven't spoken to each other since."

"Man, that's tough. I'm sorry."

She shook her head. "They weren't abusive, or mean. There just wasn't any love in the house. My dad slept around. My mother read the Bible a lot. I assume they're happier now."

"And you were happy with Jamie."

"Most of the time." She hadn't meant to say that. "I mean…every marriage has rough spots. We were good, overall."

"Except you couldn't trust him."

She put up a hand in protest. "Jamie never cheated on me."

"Not with other women. But…"

The understanding in his face allowed her to finish the sentence. "But I never could trust him with money. And, in the end, with his own life."

"A lot of people went into the military after the September 11 attacks. Maybe he felt compelled to defend his country."

"But he was my husband and I…we…needed him here. I wanted him here."

His gaze searched her face, as his warm hand covered hers. "Willa—"

"Well, there you two are!" Bev's voice carried all the way across the lobby. "I thought you'd ducked out on me completely."

In the second before he turned away, Daniel's face changed from concerned and caring to a smooth, impersonal mask. "We wouldn't do that. Is this our dance?" He stood up, and Willa was close enough to see the effort it cost him to make the smooth movement.

"That it is, cowboy." Bev grabbed his free hand. "Come on and take me in your arms."

Willa reached for the glass he still held. "Have fun, kids." Without waiting to watch them go, she picked up her champagne glass and drained it, then finished off Daniel's, too, and went to find her aunts.

The sisters stood together, watching the dancing, and both of them looked tired, maybe even despondent. Willa stepped between them and put an arm around each slender waist.

"What do you think? Is it time to go home?"

Lili looked at her and nodded. "I think so."

"Are you sure?" Rosa searched Willa's face. "Perhaps you should wait and dance some more..." She turned to scan the crowd, which parted at that moment to give them a good view of Daniel, with Bev hanging all over him. He didn't appear to mind.

"I'm definitely ready to go," Willa said.

Rosa sighed, and her shoulders drooped. "I suppose you are."

In only a matter of minutes, Willa had collected their purses and jackets and given the valet the ticket for her truck. Then the three of them slipped out of the hotel without saying goodbye to a soul.

TWO HOURS LATER, WILLA ANSWERED a knock on her front door to find Daniel standing on the veranda.

"You didn't wait until midnight," he said. "And you didn't leave a glass slipper behind."

She crossed one bare foot over the other. "I could use one. This tile is cold."

"So ask me in."

"Daniel—"

"Or not." Before she could think, or even breathe, he wrapped the tie of her flannel robe around one hand and jerked her up against him. He shut the door behind her with his other hand, and then closed both arms hard around her waist.

"This," he said in a rough voice, "is how the night was supposed to end."

Daniel's hungry mouth came down on hers, and Willa stopped fighting herself. She leaned into him, folding her arms across his shoulders, answering his demands with her own. He responded with a low growl, pressing against her until she felt the resistance of the heavy oak door at her back. She was trapped, and she didn't care.

He ran his hands over her hips and up her back to her shoulders, then combed his fingers through her hair. His lips roamed her face, her ears, and settled on the pulse under her jaw.

"I've missed you, Willa." His whisper set off shivers along her backbone. "Every night in my bed, I've missed you."

"Daniel." She cupped her hands on his cheeks and brought his mouth back to hers. The words were locked inside of her, but she used her hands to convey the feelings, dragging his shirttail out of his jeans, sweeping her palms over the ruined skin of his back.

Crazed kisses, the sweet slide of skin against skin…just the glory of wanting and being wanted sent Willa over the edge. Before she even realized what was happening, with her feet on the ground and layers of clothing still between them, her body exploded with pleasure. She clutched Daniel's shoulders, her breath caught in her throat, as waves of release rolled through her.

"Oh, God." She filled her lungs, finally, dropping her head back against the door. "I'm sorry. So sorry."

Daniel tightened his hold. "I'm not. That was fantastic."

She opened her eyes to give him a skeptical look.

He shrugged a shoulder. "I'm okay. Just touching you makes this the best day I've had in a month."

"You are a strange man."

Occupied with rebuttoning her pajama top and retying her robe, he didn't look up. "Why?"

"Most men consider their own climax the, um, main event. However long it takes."

"Or not." Daniel grinned. "I can be as selfish as the next guy. But not tonight. Not with you." Holding her shoulders, he lowered his head and kissed her gently, thoroughly, sealing the memory of his passion into her heart and soul.

Then he let her go. "Are you locked out of the house?"

Willa shook her head and opened the door.

"Then get inside and get warm. Your feet must be freezing."

She shook her head as she backed into the house. "Not at all. I feel…wonderful."

His white teeth gleamed in the night. "Good. Sleep well, Willa."

"Good night, Daniel." She watched him walk to his truck, the limp more pronounced than when he'd entered the ballroom earlier in the evening. He gave her a wave before starting the engine, and then drove away, up the road toward his house.

I should have gone with him, Willa thought.

Then she shook her head. She didn't want to sneak around, worrying about the kids or the aunts or the hands finding out. When the time had come for her to be with Daniel again, she would know.

At least tonight, she could fall asleep remembering his kisses, and his hands on her skin…a guarantee of sweet dreams.

WITH HIS BODY STILL BUZZING from the encounter with Willa, Daniel couldn't just walk into the house and fall asleep. He went for a drive, instead, visiting the pastures and the cattle he called his own. Sitting on the hood of the truck, hunched into his jacket against the chilly night, he stared at the Texas-sized sky, filled with brilliant twinkling stars, and thought about the woman he loved. How long would it take Willa to realize that she loved him, too?

A flash of light caught his eye—the twin beams of a truck's headlights coming out of the east and the darkness of the Wild Horse Desert, traveling where no road existed.

There wasn't much he could do, from this distance and with no backup, so Daniel resorted to the only weapon he had. He turned on his own truck's high beam lamps. Grinning, he watched the white beams in the distance wheel through the air, then vanish, to be replaced by winking red taillights. In seconds, the intruders had disappeared.

His grin faded, though, on the drive back to the house. No doubt about it—the rustlers had discovered his cattle. Sooner or later, they'd attempt to make off with his animals. Short of posting a twenty-four-hour guard, he wasn't sure how he would stop them.

He stood watch by himself on Sunday, sitting on that same hill in his truck, with a loaded rifle, a loaded picnic basket on the passenger seat and the latest techno-thriller paperback propped on the steering wheel to pass the time.

Monday morning, he detailed two of the hands to ride the perimeter fences, looking for any breaks or cuts. When Willa drove up with Rob, Daniel approached her side of the truck. She rolled down the window right away, he was pleased to see. Her cheeks were flushed and her smile bashful as she looked at him.

"Good morning." He propped an arm above the window. "How was your Sunday?"

"Peaceful." Finally, after all these weeks, she gave him the smile he'd set out to earn that very first evening. He nearly forgot everything else in his enjoyment of Willa's beautiful smile.

Then Rob slammed the passenger door getting out of the truck, and Daniel came back to reality.

"I'm glad to hear it," he said. "But I've got some bad news." He hated seeing her face change. "I saw headlights out beyond my fence line Saturday night. I'm pretty sure the rustlers are back."

Willa hit the steering wheel with the side of her fist. "Have you called the sheriff?"

He shook his head. "There's not much to report, so far. I saw some headlights, which could have been kids four-wheeling at night. I've got hands riding the fence line now. If they find any manmade breaks, then I'll let Sutton know."

"I guess that's reasonable." She took a deep breath. "I wish we could catch these guys and put them away."

"I'll work on that." He grazed his knuckles along her cheek and smiled when her eyes and mouth softened. "Meanwhile, don't fret about it. You've got what you wanted—a buffer on your north side."

Willa's smile faded quickly. "I wanted to tell you—Robbie won't be working on Friday."

"Getting ready for the rodeo?"

She shook her head. "*El Día de los Muertos.* The Day of the Dead, when we celebrate and remember family who are gone."

"Okay." Daniel took a breath and a step back from the truck. Somehow, the idea of Willa spending a day remembering her husband seemed to put him at a disadvantage. But he'd be a jerk to complain. "I won't expect to see either of you on Friday."

He started to turn away.

"Would you like to come?" Willa called after him, and Daniel pivoted back. "For dinner," she clarified. "Come for dinner Friday night." She looked almost as surprised at her invitation as he was.

But he wouldn't allow her time for second thoughts. "I'll be there!"

Chapter Ten

Monday afternoon, offerings started to appear on the table beneath Jamie's portrait—a fat ivory candle, a vase of brilliant orange marigolds from the garden, a soft white linen cloth and a crystal bowl of rose-scented water. Rosa's famous *pan de muerto,* a bread made with orange and anise flavoring, perfumed the whole house on Wednesday, which was Halloween. Lili prepared *atol,* a fruit drink made with corn, and set out a pitcher with glasses. Willa had ordered candies shaped like skulls from a store in town. With the addition of more candles, food and personal mementoes, plus yellow, blue and red ribbons, the Mercado family altar was prepared.

Friday evening, Willa watched as Daniel surveyed their creation. "Corona beer?" he asked with a quizzical look.

"Jamie's favorite."

"And Santa Clara Cigars?"

She shrugged. "He and his father enjoyed a smoke together now and then."

Susannah came into the parlor carrying a plate. "These are pumpkin cookies," she told Daniel. "Daddy liked them warm out of the oven, Aunt Rosa says." Willa moved some of the other items slightly so Susannah could set her cookies down. "I made them myself this year."

"And they smell delicious." Daniel snapped his fingers. "Hey—are you the person we have to thank for the boxes of treats showing up on my doorstep? Did you make the brownies, and the cookies and the pie?"

Eyes shining, cheeks flushed, Susannah nodded.

Willa crossed her arms and lifted an eyebrow. "So there hasn't been a bake sale every day at school, hmm?"

"Um…no." Susannah looked at Daniel again. "Did you like them?"

"Every last bite. Thank you very much."

Toby dashed into the room, with Robbie following more slowly. "Is it time, Mom? Is it time?"

"Almost." She noticed Robbie had stopped at the doorway, where he stood with a scowl on his face. "Come in, Roberto. Did you have something to add to the altar?"

He shook his head and turned toward the back of the house, but she reached him and grasped his shoulder before he could disappear. "What have you brought?"

His face turned dark red as he showed her the gift he carried—a pouch of tooled leather, incised with natural symbols including suns, moons, stars and birds. "Roberto, this is beautiful! Did you make it?"

Keeping his gaze averted, he nodded. "In art class."

"For your dad? Oh, son…" Tears clogged her throat. Willa put her arms around him. "He'll be so pleased," she whispered. "Place it on the altar."

Daniel watched as Rob went to put the pouch with the other offerings. The boy avoided him as if he were a rabid dog that would bite if approached too closely. Maybe he shouldn't have come tonight, after all. He hated to think his presence spoiled the occasion.

The aunts brought in a feast of food and filled his plate. "Chicken mole," Lili announced as she served him. "Jamie's favorite recipe."

"My special tamales." Rosa gave him three. "I only make them a few times a year."

After taking a bite, Daniel nodded. "Something this delicious should only be served on very special occasions."

He hadn't known exactly what to expect tonight, but he discovered that *El Día de los Muertos* was far from a sad occasion. Toby clowned around, as usual. Cheerful music played on the whole-house sound system—Jamie's pride and joy, Willa told him—and Susannah sang along in Spanish when she knew the words.

Rosa and Lili told stories about their brother, Jamie's father and his wife, and about their parents. "Papa was strict," Rosa recalled. "We got a television when they were first available, but we were not allowed to watch at all on Sundays."

"I remember when Elvis appeared on television." Lili made a prim face. "Papa wouldn't let us watch him. He said Elvis was 'rude.'" She and Rosa dissolved into laughter.

Toby looked at them with a confused expression. "Elvis? What's Elvis?"

Stories about Jamie Mercado gradually wove into the conversation. "I remember him as a toddler," Lili said. "Jamie would ride on the saddle in front of his father as he worked the cattle. By the time Jamie was six, he was herding from his own pony with the rest of the hands."

Daniel thought of his first, disastrous attempt at driving cattle.

"And the tricks he could do with that pony—Figaro was his name. Figaro would gallop across the ground and Jamie would stand up on the saddle, keeping his balance as easily as if he stood on the ground."

Willa looked at Toby, sitting on the floor by her feet. "A trick I do not want you to try under any circumstances."

Toby hung his head. "Yes, ma'am."

"I remember Daddy at a rodeo." Susannah turned to Willa.

"You were surprised, weren't you, Mama, when he entered the bull riding contest?"

"Yes, I was surprised." Willa's smile looked a little forced. "Toby was just a baby, then. I'm surprised you remember that far back, honey."

"Did he win?" Toby demanded. "Was he good?"

Willa shook her head. "Um…no. He hit the ground about a second after he left the gate. And broke his arm in the process." Her gaze connected with Daniel's for a second and then went to Robbie. "What do you remember, Roberto? You know, your dad rode with you on his saddle, just as his father had done with him."

Rob lifted one shoulder. "I don't remember that."

There was a silence, as they waited for him to add his thoughts. But Rob didn't say anything.

Because, Daniel thought, *I'm here.* For Rob, if for no one else, he was an intruder. He would say his piece and then go.

"I had three friends while I was in Iraq," he said, leaning forward a little. "Rick, Dave and Wayne. We called them The Three Stooges." He saw by the kids' blank looks that they didn't understand the reference. "They were always clowning around, pretending to beat each other up, making jokes. Nothing really special about them, or me—we were like all the other men and women over there, trying to do a good job for our country and for the people of Iraq.

"Each of those guys, though, was a hero in one way or another. I saw Rick save two little boys from a sniper attack by lying on top of them and shielding their bodies with his own. Dave refused to leave an old woman in a building he knew was going to be bombed any minute, even when she fought him every step of the way as he pulled her out."

He took a deep breath. "And Wayne…well, Wayne was driving our vehicle the day I got hurt. I was lying in the road right next to the burning car and Wayne used the one arm he had left to drag me far enough away to be out of range when the gas tank exploded. He went back for Rick…" Swallowing hard, he managed to finish. "But they didn't get away in time."

He met each pair of eyes in the room, Rob's last. "I'm sure that Jamie Mercado was the same kind of hero. He would have similar stories to tell, except he'd be embarrassed to let anyone know how many people he'd helped, how many lives he'd saved."

Pushing against the arms of his chair, Daniel got to his feet. "You are rightfully proud of the man your family has lost, and right to celebrate his life. I appreciate the chance to share that with you." He nodded to Lili and Rosa. "Thank you for a delicious meal, ladies. Have a good night." To Willa, he said, "Don't get up. I'll let myself out."

She followed him, though, all the way out to the veranda. "That was a lovely thing to say."

"Your husband was a decent man." He grinned and shrugged. "With a few flaws."

"Like everyone." Willa nodded. "You've helped me see him in a more balanced light."

"That's good." For Jamie, anyway. Daniel wasn't sure whether he'd helped or hurt his own cause. He turned toward the truck, parked nearby. "Have a good evening."

"Daniel." Her hand on his arm brought him back around to face her. When he looked into her face, there was no doubt that she was waiting to be kissed.

Aware of the house windows, he kept his hands at his sides, saying everything with just the press of his mouth over hers. That seemed to be enough—they were both panting when he raised his head.

"Rodeo tomorrow," Willa said, smiling. "We'll see you bright and early."

Driving home, Daniel decided he would celebrate *El Día de los Muertos* every year from now on.

AFTER A WEEK SPENT WORKING around Robbie's defiant silence, Daniel was relieved when Willa asked him if her aunts could ride with him to the rodeo. He half expected the ladies to be wearing their matching flowered dresses, but when he pulled into the drive at the Mercado house, they waited for him on the veranda in neat jeans and Western boots, with long-sleeved shirts worn under colorful vests.

"Are you sure you two aren't part of the show?" He helped Rosa into the front passenger seat with a hand on her elbow, then assisted Lili into the back. "Do they have a best-dressed cowgirl contest?"

Rosa clucked her tongue at him. "You're a flatterer, Daniel. No wonder Willa likes you."

He couldn't help grinning at the thought that Willa liked him. She responded to him, sure…they'd had chemistry from that first moment in the lawyer's office. But at this point he was grateful for any evidence hinting at more than just a physical connection.

At the fairgrounds, the bare bones of fences, corrals and bleachers set on a wide dirt plain had been fleshed out with flags, advertising banners, animals and people. Carts and trailers and tents were set up to sell everything from dream catchers to Polish sausage, with shoppers crowding the aisles between them. Country music blared out of the public address system, punctuated by an announcer counting down the minutes until the official start of the rodeo.

They found Willa's truck and horse trailer parked in the competitor's lot. Susannah was giving her pony a final brush as they approached.

"That horse shines as bright as gold," Daniel told her. "I've never seen an animal so clean."

She flashed him a smile. "I gave him a bath yesterday, but

then he rolled during the night, so I had to wash him off again this morning. He's probably never been this clean in his life."

"You look terrific, too." To complement her horse, Susannah's chaps were royal-blue with gold fringe. Her blouse was the same blue, and she wore a blue hat that made her long black braid shine. "Where's your—"

A hand slipped inside Daniel's elbow. He looked down, starting to smile at Willa…but it was Bev Drummond who stood beside him.

He had to force himself to finish the smile. "Fancy meeting you here."

"I'm so glad you decided to come." Her other hand, with its long red fingernails, came to rest on top of his arm. "Susannah's going to make us all proud today. I just know it."

The girl gave a nervous smile and continued to groom her horse.

Bev squeezed Daniel's arm. "Let's take a stroll through the booths. I haven't had my breakfast yet, and there's an elephant ear pastry over there calling my name."

He didn't have an excuse to stay—he couldn't do much to help Susannah. Willa and Toby were nowhere in sight. The aunts had already wandered off to do some shopping.

"Sure. I could use some coffee, myself." He looked at Susannah. "We'll be back in a few minutes."

But Bev had other plans. She dragged him from vendor to vendor, examining jewelry and knickknacks, asking his opinion of items he couldn't care less about. Just as he was about to suggest they head back to the trailer, the loudspeaker above his head crackled.

"In five minutes, the Grand Parade opening the Zapata County Rodeo will commence. Spectators, grab a drink and something to eat, then settle in for a great day of exciting rodeo action!"

"Let's find ourselves a seat," Bev said, clamping down on his arm again and dragging him toward the arena.

Daniel had long since gotten tired of being hauled around like a toddler. He started to dig in his heels and reclaim his arm...but then he caught sight of Willa, Toby and Robbie, also heading for the bleachers.

"Look," he said. "There's Willa." Changing direction, he pulled Bev along with him, pretending he didn't hear her squawk of protest.

He caught up with the Mercados at the corner of the grandstand. Toby saw him first. "Major Trent! The rodeo is about to start!"

At Toby's shout, Willa turned, her first expression a surprised grin. Then she saw Bev, clamped onto Daniel's arm, and the grin faded to a polite smile. "Hi, Bev. Is Susannah ready to ride?" She flicked a glance at Daniel, without meeting his eyes.

"We left her giving Lustre a final brush." Bev flipped her long red hair in back of her shoulders. "We should find a place to sit or we'll be standing along the wall."

Willa nodded. "My aunts were going to stake out some territory on the benches." She turned and led the way through the crowd, past the ticket booth and then up the side of the bleachers to where Lili and Rosa sat on either end of an empty stretch of bench, in perfect viewing position. Rob filed in to sit next to Rosa, followed by Willa. Daniel thought he could take the space beside her, but then Toby scooted ahead of him, to sit next to his mother. Somehow Bev slipped in after Toby, and Daniel ended up on her other side, with Lili on his right. He grinned at Willa's aunt, winked at Bev and kept his disappointed sigh to himself.

The Grand Parade started a moment later as the day's competitors rode their horses into the arena and loped around the perimeter—bronc and bull riders, calf ropers, steer wrestlers and clowns and, finally, the barrel racers, all wearing their flashy chaps, their show clothes and their good hats. Susannah caught sight of her family and waved as she rode past.

Last came a trio of gray horses mounted by pretty young women wearing red, white and blue. As the other riders lined up down the center of the field, the color guard circled the arena to display the American flag, with the Texas flag and the flag of Zapata County just behind. Section by section the members of the audience got to their feet, and the national anthem came over the loudspeaker. Listening, Daniel swallowed tears, as he always did. He wasn't surprised that each member of the Mercado family knew every word of the song.

The anthem ended with a cheer from spectators and competitors alike, and the rodeo got underway. Toby leaned over Bev to talk to Daniel. "First is the bareback riding. Then saddle broncs, calf roping and steer wrestling. Then they set up for the barrel racers, and the bull riding is last." He glanced back at his mother, who was saying something to Rosa. "I'm gonna ride bulls one day," the boy said in a stage whisper. "Don't tell my mom yet."

Daniel nodded. "I won't." But when he glanced over Toby's head, he could see from Willa's face that she'd heard. He winked at her, sharing her amused apprehension.

Toby hopped up at the end of the bareback riding and went to the concession stand for popcorn. After the saddle broncs, he wanted a hot dog, and Rob went with him—stepping across Daniel without a word. Halfway through the calf-roping, Toby stood up again. "I'm going to the bathroom, Mom. And then I need some lunch."

"How can you need something else to eat?" Willa stared at him, pretending dismay. "You've been eating all morning!"

He shrugged and grinned, knowing she was teasing. "I'm a growing boy. What can I say? Oh, yeah…" He snapped his fingers. "I need some money."

"Of course, you do." Willa handed him a folded bill. "Put that in your pocket now—don't carry it around in your hand."

"Okay, okay." He did as he was told. "I'll be back in a little while."

His mother shook her head as he eased along the bench. "He'll be seven feet tall, if he keeps eating like this."

"Or seven feet wide," Bev said, with a laugh.

Daniel looked at the redhead without comment. What she saw in his face, though, gave her second thoughts. "N-not really, of course. He never stops moving—he needs all the food he can eat."

As the last of the calf ropers left the arena, Daniel noticed Willa scanning the stands, looking for Toby. She said something to Rob, who stood up and gazed around, shaking his head. In a few minutes, Lili and Rosa were both on the lookout, as well.

Daniel leaned across Bev and touched Willa's arm to get her attention. "You think Toby should have been back by now?"

Willa shrugged. "I would have thought so…but sometimes he wanders off on his own." She was calm, but her eyebrows were drawn together in worry.

"Why don't I go look for him?"

"No, don't bother. I'm sure he'll be back."

"It's not a bother. I need to stretch my legs, anyway. I'll just look around and then send him back so you'll know he's okay."

She couldn't hide the relief. "Thank you. That would be nice."

As he stood up, Bev picked up her purse. "I'll come with you."

Daniel put a hand on her shoulder. "That's okay. You can't really follow me into the men's restroom." He gave her a grin. "I'll be back shortly."

"Well," Bev said, her voice high with irritation. "I could have waited for him outside!"

Willa kept her gaze on the action in the arena. "Maybe he wanted a few minutes alone."

"So he goes after a ten-year-old?"

After a morning spent listening to Bev play rodeo expert, Willa was having trouble keeping her temper. "He's doing me a favor, Bev. Toby's been gone more than half an hour."

"Maybe you should have gone to look for him."

"But I can't get into the men's restroom, either."

After a moment, Bev slid down the bench toward Willa. "Listen, girlfriend, I think we need to get this settled, right now, before he comes back."

"Get what settled?"

"You may not realize it, but I'm very interested in Major Daniel Trent. I think we could have some good times together, maybe even on a permanent basis."

Willa folded her arms over her chest. "Oh, really?"

"Yes. I know he's your neighbor, and I'm sure you see a lot of him, one way or another. But I'm asking you now, as a friend, to back off."

"You think Daniel's interested in a relationship with you?"

"I think he's trying to decide—you or me. Which is why I want you to leave him alone."

Willa had to laugh. "It's that simple, is it? I leave, and Daniel falls for you?"

"Yes, it is."

"Oh, Beverley, you're priceless." Willa wiped her eyes, but she couldn't stop giggling. "Love doesn't come with an on/off switch. And it's not either/or. If Daniel is in love with you, being around me won't make the least bit of difference."

Bev rolled her eyes. "What do you know? You've been married once, to your childhood sweetheart. I learned the hard way—with two husbands and a bunch of boyfriends."

"Or maybe you didn't learn anything at all."

Bev stared at her in fury. "You bitch."

"Here's the thing, Bev." Willa put a hand on her former friend's knee. "I think I could move to the other side of the planet, and it wouldn't change the way Daniel feels about you in the least. But for the record, no. I won't back off. Find yourself another trophy, girlfriend. This one's mine."

While she was dealing with the fear and exhilaration of having admitted so much, Bev got to her feet and sidestepped to the aisle. She turned back before starting down the steps. "Just so you know, your daughter couldn't ride her way out of a paper bag."

Willa simply waved her away. Susannah would prove that comment a lie when she streaked into the arena a little bit later this afternoon.

Now that Bev was out of the way, Willa wanted Daniel to come back, wanted to share the fun and excitement of the rodeo with the man she'd practically declared her private property. But he'd been gone almost twenty minutes, and Toby hadn't returned.

"I'm going to look for them," she told Rosa, Robbie and Lili. "You three stay here."

ROBBIE HEARD THE WHOLE conversation between his mom and Miss Beverley. He'd been afraid of this. Mom had decided she liked Daniel Trent enough to fight with her friend over him.

Wasn't there any way to stop this disaster from getting worse?

He was thinking so hard that the light tap on his shoulder made him jump. He looked to his left, where Aunt Rosa sat smiling at him.

"What are you pondering so deeply?" As he stared at her, she started looking worried. "Is something wrong, Robbie?"

Would talking things over with Aunt Rosa do any good? He doubted it. "I think Mom's getting interested in Mr. Trent."

"Is that a bad thing?"

"She said he would only be here till Christmas."

"But he seems to be settling into ranch work and ranch life pretty well. Maybe she was wrong."

"She doesn't really know anything about him."

"I suspect she's learning, as we all are. Do you know something about Major Trent we should be aware of?"

He wished he had thought ahead of time to make something up. Something really bad, like killing people. Or dogs. "He probably shot up a lot of people in the war."

"That could be true. Unfortunately, war often demands that kind of sacrifice."

"He might have that mental problem…PMST or whatever."

"PTSD, you mean. Post-traumatic stress disorder."

"Right. He might freak out sometime and think we're all the enemy and shoot us with those guns he has."

Rosa put a hand on his shoulder. "Or he might just take up more of your mother's time and attention than you're ready to hand over."

Robbie gave a snort. "I'm not a baby. But I think we're good the way we are. We don't need anybody else."

"Maybe your mother feels differently." His great-aunt sighed. "Your mother's a young woman, Robbie. You and Susannah and Toby will grow up and find your own lives one day. Shouldn't she have someone special of her own to share the rest of her life?"

"She'll have all of us, just like you do, and be happy like you are."

"I'll tell you the truth," Rosa said, tucking her fingers into the bend of his elbow. "I once loved a boy—many years ago, now. He loved me, too. But he went to war and was killed there." She sighed. "I love you and your brother and sister and Lili and your mother very, very much. But if I could have had a life with him...that would have been happiness. The kind of happiness I wish for your mother, and for you."

She turned back to watch the steer wrestling, and Robbie saw her dab at her eyes with her fingers.

Great. She's crying. Trent was making trouble for all of them. Butting in where he didn't belong, making Suze all mushy and hard to talk to. Mom had started off marking the days on her calendar until he left, but then she'd stopped, as if she didn't want to know anymore.

Robbie was still keeping track. And all he wanted as a gift for *Navidad* this year was to see the cloud of dust as Daniel Trent disappeared from their lives forever.

Chapter Eleven

Daniel checked out the portable latrines standing within sight of the arena and strolled down the main food aisle without finding Toby. Worry started curling in his gut—these Zapata County folks looked friendly enough, but a kid could easily vanish in a crowd like this.

On his way to request the announcer to call Toby over the loudspeaker, he spotted a concrete block hut that also housed restrooms and detoured to check them out.

The old building smelled of mildew and urine. The men's room was L-shaped, with urinals along one arm, stalls and sinks opposite each other on the other. Two teenagers stood at the sinks, washing their hands—his first clue that something wasn't right. Of the three stalls, two had no door. The third was closed.

Daniel went to the farthest urinal and turned his back on the teenagers. He heard the shuffle of boots on concrete.

"Hand it over," one of them said, his voice a low growl.

"Throw it out here, kid." That accent sounded like New York, not Texas. "Then we'll let you go."

Returning to the row of stalls, Daniel saw the teenagers crouched near the floor, trying to reach under the closed door. Whoever was inside kept kicking at their hands and arms with sharp-toed black boots. Toby's boots.

Daniel cleared his throat. "Toby? You okay?"

The teenagers jerked their heads up.

"I'm okay," Toby yelled from behind the stall door. "They want my money and I'm not gonna give it to them."

"No, I wouldn't expect you to." The teenagers wanted to run, but Daniel stood in the doorway, blocking their exit. "Pretty impressive, ganging up on a ten-year-old."

"He's a wimp." The older one tried to bluster his way out. "He must be, if all he's got is a gimp like you to protect him." He glanced at his friend. "We can handle this one, Joey. No problem."

Daniel circled the tip of his cane out in front of him. "You can try."

The kids rushed him like linebackers. He took one out at the knees with his cane and caught the other in the face with his elbow. Then he stood looking down at them as they lay moaning on the floor.

"I see why you two pick on the little guys." He held out his hand to Toby, who had come out of the stall. "Let's go find your mom, buddy. We'll leave Dumb and Dumber to recover."

Outside, though, he stopped and put his fingers under Toby's chin. "Are you okay? Did they hurt you?"

The boy shook his head. "Nope. They couldn't get to me in the stall with the door locked."

"How did they know you had money?"

Toby looked down at his feet. "I unzipped my jeans to...you know...pee...and the bill fell out of my pocket. I picked it up quick, but they started bugging me for the money, so I ran into the stall and locked the door."

"That was good thinking." Daniel patted him on the back. "Your mom is probably wondering what happened to both of us. Let's find her, get some grub and go back to see your sister win the barrel race."

They met Willa in the middle of the food aisle. Daniel saw

her first, saw the anxiety in her eyes and the tension in her shoulders. Then he had the pleasure of seeing all the stress wiped away by a smile when he called her name. "Willa! I've got him."

Before Willa could even begin a lecture, Toby launched into his story. "You shoulda seen it, Mom. These two creeps were trying to get my money, only I locked myself in the stall over there in the old bathroom so they couldn't get to me, and they kept reaching under the door, but then Daniel came and they rushed at him but he just knocked 'em down without even breathing hard. It was really awesome, Mom."

Willa gazed at her son in silence for a minute. "Well, that was quite an adventure." Then she looked at Daniel. "Thank you very much. I don't know whether Toby will survive to adulthood without you to keep him safe."

Daniel would have liked to say something casual. He was pretty sure a marriage proposal didn't qualify. "No problem," he said finally, still holding her gaze. "I'm glad I could help."

"Man, I'm starved." Toby tugged at Willa's arm. "Can we please get something to eat now?"

Willa looked away from the emotions she saw in Daniel's serious face. "Sure. Everybody's hungry at this point. Let's take lunch back to the stands."

Carrying fried chicken, drinks and chips, they made their way to the arena, where Toby's return was celebrated with a cheer from Robbie and applause from the aunts. This time he sat between his mother and brother, leaving the space on Willa's other side free for Daniel.

"Where's Bev?" he asked between bites of chicken.

Willa considered telling him the truth but couldn't quite find the nerve. "She usually stays with her riders before the race. Last-minute advice and all that."

"That's just as well. We didn't buy enough chips." He held up a bag. "There's only one left."

"Somebody will have to share."

Daniel looked over at the boys, who had already finished their bags. "I don't think it will be them."

The two of them shared the bag of chips, brushing fingers as they reached in together. Daniel's thigh settled against her leg, and Willa didn't move away. Her heart was tripping in her chest and she couldn't catch her breath. She hadn't been this happy in years.

Once the steer wrestlers finished up, the clowns did their routine, and then little kids chased a bunch of squealing piglets through the dirt. When the laughter and the applause died down, the announcer said, "And now, ladies and gents, one of the highlights of the Zapata County Rodeo is fixing to get started—the ever-popular barrel racing event! First up this afternoon is Darcy Layton on Good To Go."

"She's Susannah's main competition," Willa told Daniel. "They've both been training with Bev."

Holding her breath, she saw Darcy bolt into the arena on her neat bay quarterhorse. Their performance was flawless and their time phenomenal. "Fourteen point nine-three-four seconds," came over the loudspeaker. "A terrific time for Miss Darcy Layton."

They sat through ten riders before Susannah's run finally arrived. "Next to go, Miss Susannah Mercado riding Golden Lustre."

Toby and Rob surged to their feet. "Yay, Susannah!"

"Rip it, Suze!"

Willa sat forward, pulse pounding. Susannah's run around the barrels was a blur, too fast to follow.

Toby cheered again. "That was a great one, Mom."

She nodded. "She didn't knock down a barrel, at least."

"What happens if you knock down a barrel?" Daniel squeezed her fingers gently, and she realized they'd never unlinked their hands.

"Um…" Her mind wouldn't work for a moment.

"Five-second penalty," Toby supplied.

"That's right. Five seconds."

"You're not gonna believe this, folks." The announcer cleared his throat. "It almost never happens. But Susannah Mercado's time was fourteen point nine-three-four seconds. We've got a tie going on!"

"Will they have a tie-breaker?" Daniel asked.

"I guess so." Willa shook her head. "I've never seen a tie before."

The tension increased for the Mercado crowd with each rider.

Fifteen point one-six-two seconds. Sixteen point four-three-three. Fifteen point zero-zero-three.

Willa blew out a long breath. "That was close."

Fifteen point two-four-five.

Daniel shifted on the hard aluminum seat. "One more to go."

"Are you uncomfortable?" Willa glanced at his right leg, stretched underneath the bench in front of them. "We could find a place to stand." She hardly thought about his injuries anymore—the cane had become practically invisible to her eyes.

He shook his head. "I'm fine. Here we go."

The whole audience seemed to be holding its collective breath during the final ride. Willa kept her gaze on the clock posted above the announcer's booth. She knew the outcome even before horse and rider crossed the finish line.

"That's an upset, folks," the announcer said in an awed voice. "Miss Terri Vance scored a time of fourteen point nine-three-three seconds. Let's give her a big hand, ladies and gentlemen. She's the winner by exactly one one-thousandth of a second!"

Susannah smiled brightly as she received a trophy for her second-place finish in the barrel race. She gave the crowd a big wave as she rode Lustre out of the arena, leaving the winner to take a victory lap to enthusiastic applause.

Willa blew out a long breath. "I should go talk to her. I know she's upset."

"I'll go." Rob stood up and edged his way to the steps without waiting for Willa's permission. Nobody else on the Mercado bench said a word. The whole family had taken a blow, though she wasn't sure why. Susannah had won and lost other races. This one had just seemed more important for some reason.

"Maybe we should go home now," Toby suggested.

She looked at him in surprise. "But we haven't seen the bull riding. That's your favorite event."

"I know. But we've been here a long time and I'm tired." He shrugged. "We could watch a movie after supper. That would be okay with me."

She wondered if he was getting sick and almost put a hand on his forehead to check his temperature but realized just in time that he'd be embarrassed.

Instead, she turned to Daniel. "I guess we're going to take Susannah home. But if you want to stay, please do. We can fit Rosa and Lili in my truck."

She wasn't really surprised when he shook his head. "That's okay. I've seen it before—you're crazy, you sit on top of a crazy animal, you fall off." He grinned. "I can wait for the video."

Willa gave him a grateful smile and turned to pick up the trash from their meal. "Well, then, let's go home."

When they reached her truck, they found Lustre loaded in the trailer and ready to go. Susannah and Robbie stood face-to-face by the truck, and they seemed to be arguing. When Susannah caught sight of her family, though, she turned away from her twin. "I was just coming to join you all."

Willa put an arm around her daughter's shoulders. "We decided we weren't all that interested in the bull riding. What do you say we go on home, fire up the grill and cook some burgers, then put on one of our favorite movies and fall asleep on the couch?"

Susannah sagged against her side. "That sounds good to me."

With the horse trailer shut up tight, Lili and Rosa took their usual places in her truck. Toby turned to Willa. "Can I ride home with Major Trent, Mom?"

"Um…" She glanced at Daniel. "Would it be a problem to drop him off?"

"Not at all. I'll enjoy the company."

Susannah glanced at Robbie, who gave her a stern look. "Hey Mom," she said, "can I ride with Major Trent, too?"

Willa saw Robbie's outraged glare and wondered what was going on between them. "I guess so, sweetie. We'll see you at home. Thanks, Daniel."

He gave her a wink and a salute. Watching the trio walk toward Daniel's truck, she saw his hand resting lightly on Toby's shoulder while he tilted his head toward Susannah, listening to something she was saying. The man was terrific dad material.

"Daniel's going to make a wonderful father," Rosa said, as Willa cranked the truck engine.

Willa didn't respond. But Robbie slammed the back passenger door with a force that rocked the entire vehicle. She stared at him through the rearview mirror.

What had gotten into her son?

TOBY FELL ASLEEP IN THE back seat almost before they left the fairgrounds and woke up just as they turned into the Blue Moon gates. "We're already home? That didn't take very long."

"You were asleep, silly," his sister said. "Like always."

"I was resting my eyes." Toby yawned, then sat up straighter. "Man, I'm hungry. I'm gonna eat three burgers for supper. Hey, Daniel, you're staying to eat with us, right? Mom said we could have a movie afterward. We've got the complete set of the *Star Wars* videos. Do you like *Star Wars?* We could start with the first one and watch them straight through to the end. Or we could watch the *Ring* trilogy—we've got that, too. It wouldn't be quite so long, unless we watched the extended version. That's about eight hours."

They reached the house before Toby ran out of suggestions for the night's entertainment. Willa had stopped in the drive ahead of them to let Rosa and Lili out before going on to the barn to park the trailer and put Lustre in her corral.

Susannah looked over at Daniel as she opened her door. "Thanks, Major Trent. I'm glad you came with us today."

"Me, too. I enjoyed watching you ride."

She slipped out of the truck and opened the back door for Toby, who hopped down and raced to catch up with his great-aunts as they entered the house. Daniel gazed after them all for a moment, then turned to put the truck in gear. He jumped in surprise when he saw Willa standing right beside the driver's window.

"Thanks for bringing them home," she said, when he lowered the glass. "I'd forgotten how quiet a drive can be without Toby."

He shared her grin. "He fell asleep, so we had a fairly quiet trip, ourselves." Taking a risk, he brushed his fingertips across her cheek. "I appreciate your letting me come along today. I had a terrific time."

As his hand left her face, she caught and held it with hers. "Especially the dust-up with a couple of teenaged thugs in the bathroom?"

Her gesture left him nearly speechless. "Um…yeah."

"Can you stay for dinner?"

Daniel gazed at her, his mind blank.

"By the time we get the horse settled and the trailer un-hitched, Lili and Rosa will have the food ready." When he still didn't say anything, she stepped back, taking her hand from his. Her smile faded. "But if you've got other plans—"

"No. No." He barely kept himself from leaning out the window to jerk her close again. "That'll be great. Dinner sounds great. I'm happy to stay. Really." Taking a deep breath, he recovered his control. "Can I do something to help? At the barn? In the kitchen?"

"Lili and Rosa only allow the kids to help in the kitchen. So I guess you'll have to come to the barn with me."

With Rob and Susannah doing most of the work, the chores at the barn took only a few minutes. As Willa had promised, the hamburgers were ready for the grill when they returned to the house. They cooked and ate in the central courtyard around which the house was built, where tall live oak trees shaded a tiled fountain as big as some swimming pools. A riot of flowers brought color and perfume to the garden.

"I can't believe it's November." Daniel gestured at the beauty around them. "How much longer will the weather hold?"

"Days, a couple of weeks at the outside." Willa took a sip of lemonade. "Most years, the rains start toward the end of the month."

"Does it ever get downright cold?"

"By most standards, no. But sometimes, in January and February, the temperatures drop. We get ice storms, occasionally. One year, we even had real snow."

"I'd better stock up on warm clothes, just in case," Daniel said. Willa held his gaze for a long moment, but she didn't say a word to suggest he wouldn't be around to suffer through a January ice storm.

Much to Toby's disappointment, Daniel decided to leave without watching a movie. "Trouble is home by himself," Daniel explained. "Nate left several hours ago, so I'd better get up there and keep him company."

"You could bring him here, and he could watch the movie, too!"

Daniel glanced at Willa's frown. "I don't think so. Maybe sometime you can watch a movie at my place with Trouble."

"Okay." Toby spent a moment in the role of the pouting child, but the opening music from the film distracted him. "See you later," he called as he ran down the hall.

Willa walked Daniel to the front door. "When she got home, Susannah seemed less distressed than I expected her to be. Did you have something to do with that?"

"We talked a little, about winning and losing. She did most of the work. Very smart, your daughter."

"I've always thought so." They stepped out onto the veranda, where the night had turned cool. Willa rubbed her hands up and down her arms. "Brr. The daytime temperatures don't change all that much, but it gets practically cold at night."

"You should have a jacket." Daniel closed the distance between them, putting his arms around her and shielding her from the wind. "Or something."

Willa let herself be folded close. She looked up into his face. "Or something."

He took that for the invitation it was, and bent to put his mouth on hers. The kiss was warm and sweet, tasting of the coffee ice cream they'd enjoyed for dessert. Willa melted into him, savoring the comfort as his body enclosed her. They could have been together for years, so familiar and welcome was his scent, the feel of him surrounding her. Passion was there, too, a banked fire at the bottom of this warm glow. Given a breath of air, the flame would ignite, consuming them both.

She drew back, instead. "Good night, Daniel."

"Good night." He kissed her forehead, squeezed her shoulders gently, his palms warm. In another minute, he was gone.

Willa stood for a while after his taillights disappeared, smiling to herself, treasuring the physical pleasures of being a woman. Just as she turned to go inside, a footstep sounded on the gravel of the driveway.

Peering into the darkness, she recognized the silhouette of her older son. "Robbie? What in the world are you doing out here? I thought you were watching the movie."

"How can you let him touch you like that?"

She fell back a step, she was so startled. "I beg your pardon?"

"You let him hold you. You let him kiss you." He stood with his feet set wide, his fists clenched at his sides and his shoulders rigid. "Why are you doing it? What about Dad?"

Willa swallowed the urge to shout back. "Your dad is gone, Robbie. He's dead. You know that."

"But this is *his* ranch. You're *his* wife. We don't need that guy here. We don't need anybody else."

Willa stepped forward and put a hand on his shoulder. "Nobody can replace your dad, son. I know that. I wouldn't even try."

He stepped backward, out of her reach. "Maybe you aren't. But Trent is. He's trying to take over. Don't you see it?"

"No, I don't. Look, you know I didn't want to sell the land. But we need the money, Robbie. Daniel Trent is honest, at least. He's willing to help out if he can, and he's willing to learn what he doesn't know. We were lucky to get him as a neighbor, instead of someone who would let his cattle knock down fences, who would dam up the creeks we depend on and try to take over more than he deserves."

"You said he wouldn't stay. You said he'd be gone by Christmas."

"I know I did. I didn't see how he could succeed."

"He *is* succeeding, though, because we're helping him. I'm up there every day doing work that makes it easier for him to stick around. Did you think about that, when you decided to punish me? You're making *me* help him keep part of our land."

She hadn't thought of it that way. "I'm sorry the situation is painful for you. But you made a bad decision when you stole that gun. You made another one when you took it to school. And you lied to me about it, Roberto. You wanted me to believe that Daniel encouraged you, showed you the weapon and told you stories about the war. Did you think there would be no consequences to lying and stealing? Was I supposed to look the other way?"

"You were supposed to get mad and get rid of him!"

Willa felt as if she'd had the breath knocked out of her. "You made up this scheme just to get Daniel to leave? Why would you do something so…so underhanded and cruel?"

"To protect us. Protect you." He held out his arms, as if to embrace the land around them. "To protect this place."

"From Daniel? What are you afraid of?"

"He wants the Blue Moon, Mom. And he's using you, and the rest of the family, to get it."

She lowered her voice, trying to soften the edge of hysteria she could hear in Robbie's. "Son, you and Susannah and Toby are Mercados, born and raised. This ranch will always belong to you."

"Maybe you really think that." His tone only sharpened. "But he's going to get it all when he fools you into marrying him. He'll take over the Blue Moon, and you won't be able to stop him."

She wished she could tell him she'd never thought about marrying Daniel, but that would be a lie. Sometimes, in the middle of the night, she'd let herself think about how lovely it would be to have him there to hold her. She'd fantasized about how strong he was, how steady and calm, and how good it would be to have his support as she managed the Blue Moon. "You're wrong, Robbie. I would never deprive you of your rights to this land."

"I've seen the way you look at him. He'll be so convincing, you'll do whatever he wants, little by little…until one day, everything Dad worked for, everything he loved, will belong to Daniel Trent." He stopped, and she could hear his breathing, harsh in the darkness. "You'll probably even let him adopt us. We won't even *be* Mercados anymore!"

"Roberto, no—" She reached for him, horrified.

Before she could touch him, Robbie spun on his heel and took off at a run in the direction of the barn. Willa didn't want him out alone in the dark, especially not with rustlers prowling the desert. But if she went after him, he wouldn't relent. And she couldn't wrestle her son to the ground—he outweighed her by twenty pounds or more.

She sat down in one of the rockers on the veranda to wait. The night grew cold, and she went inside for a blanket to wrap around her shoulders, then returned to her post. At midnight, Robbie hadn't returned. Shivering, dozing off and on, Willa startled into complete wakefulness at 2:00 a.m. and stumbled into the house. Toby and Susannah had, indeed, fallen asleep in front of the television. They looked comfortable enough, stretched out on the two big couches, so she made sure they were warm enough, turned off the TV and the lights and left them alone.

She walked down the hall to the bedrooms, afraid of what she'd find when she reached Robbie's room. If he wasn't back, she'd have to go look for him…

But the door was locked, with a band of light showing underneath. The bass line of his music vibrated through the panel. He'd returned and barricaded himself in his private realm. Not a terrific outcome to their argument, but at least she knew he was safe.

Willa couldn't stop shaking, though, even wearing her warmest pajamas, with two pairs of socks on her feet and two extra blankets on top of the covers on her bed. She lay there, shivering, for more than an hour, before finally surrendering to the need building inside her. Without turning on the light, she fumbled for the phone by her bed.

Daniel picked up on the second ring. "H'lo?" His drowsy voice brought tears to her eyes. She couldn't speak.

"Willa?" His guess provoked a sob, which she barely choked back. "Willa, are you okay?"

"Yes," she gasped. "Everything's okay. I just—"

"What time is it?" The bed clothes rustled as he rolled over. "What's keeping you awake at three in the morning?"

"It's nothing. An argument with Robbie."

"He was pretty tense all day."

"Yes."

"Maybe talking it out will make things better."

"I'm not so sure."

He accepted her concern without argument. "You'll work it out. Grieving doesn't happen all at once. You go through stages. But most people come to acceptance eventually. I think Rob will."

"I hope so." She could feel her fingers and toes again. Daniel's warm voice was melting the ice in her veins.

"You need to take care of yourself, too, you know."

His words broke something deep inside of her. She buried her face in the pillow, hoping to stifle the sound of her sobs.

"Willa…"

Chapter Twelve

When Willa woke up again, the morning sun shone brightly through the blinds on her windows…she'd obviously slept through her usual 5:00 a.m. alarm. The phone rested on the pillow beside her head. She'd cried herself to sleep, with Daniel on the other end of the line. And she'd slept better than she could remember having done in weeks.

He didn't answer his phone when she pressed Redial—he'd be outside working, as she should be. What did you say to a man you'd left hanging on the phone while you sobbed and snored?

Once showered and dressed, Willa hurried to the kitchen, planning to breakfast on coffee and a piece of toast before starting her belated chores. She stopped dead on the threshold, though, and let the swinging door hit her in the rear end.

"'Morning, Mom!" Toby waved a piece of toast in her direction. "Susannah and I fed and watered the horses already."

"I'll make you an omelet." Lili got up from the table and went to the stove. "Spinach, cheese and bacon?"

"Um…sure." She couldn't quite focus, couldn't quit staring at the man across the room. "Has, um, anyone seen Robbie?"

"He left a cereal bowl in the sink and a note saying he was going out on Tar for a long ride." Rosa smiled at her. "And, as you see, Daniel finally took us up on our offer to stop by for breakfast one morning."

He sat between Toby and Susannah, calmly buttering his toast. But his gaze searched her face as he looked up. "How are you today?" Did everyone hear the meaning behind his words, or was she extra-sensitive?

"I'm good," she told him, realizing she meant it. Lili poured coffee into the mug at her regular seat and Willa sat down. "I don't usually sleep this late."

"Well, it is Sunday," Rosa pointed out. "There's no harm in taking a Sunday off now and then."

"But—"

"In fact, we were just talking about making up a picnic lunch for you and Daniel to take with you on your ride today."

Willa choked on her coffee. "Ride?"

"I thought we could ride the fences on my place and yours," he said. "Check the herds."

"So you really would be working." Lili set a plate in front of her, laden with a large omelet and a healthy pile of hash brown potatoes. "The weather is supposed to be cool and clear."

Resistance would be futile. "What can I say?" Willa toasted Daniel and then her family with coffee. "Here's to a full day's work."

As they had every Sunday of their lives except when they were sick, Rosa and Lili left the Blue Moon at ten-fifteen and drove into Zapata to attend church. They brought Toby and Susannah with them—their youth group would be spending the afternoon giving puppet shows and enjoying a pizza party with some of the town's disadvantaged children.

Once the van carrying the group had left the parking lot after the service, Lili and Rosa turned toward their own car...and found Nate Hernandez parked right next to them.

Rosa glanced at her sister, who had started to blush. That meant Lili would be feeling too shy to speak to the man. So she would have to.

"Good morning, Nate." She kept her hand at Lili's elbow and drew her forward as they approached the foreman. "Isn't the weather wonderful?"

He removed his hat and gave them a courtly nod. "'Mornin', ladies. Doesn't get any better than this. How are you today, Miss Lili? Miss Rosa?"

Rosa waited, giving Lili the opportunity to answer. "Fine, Nate," she murmured after a hesitation. "How are you?"

"Real good, now that I've seen you two pretty ladies."

A pause fell as the two of them gazed everywhere but at each other. Again, Rosa waited, until she thought she might scream in frustration.

"Are you working today, Nate?"

"No, ma'am. The boss insists I take Sundays off, even if I don't want 'em."

"He and Willa were going to ride the fence lines today on the Blue Moon and-and the New Moon," Lili said unexpectedly. "You shouldn't worry about not being there one day a week."

Nate looked almost as surprised as Rosa at Lili's speech. "Well, that's good to know. The boss is the one who really needs a day off, though. He works himself hard enough during the day. I think he's been spending nights keeping watch on the pastures, trying to catch them rustlers. Cain't be getting a whole lot of sleep."

After having said so much, both Lili and Nate relapsed into silence.

When a figure across the parking lot caught her attention, Rosa made an instantaneous decision. "I'm going home alone," she declared, pulling the car keys out of her purse. She pushed them into Lili's open hands. "You two should find somewhere to have lunch while the children are busy with the youth group.

Either you'll figure out a way to talk to each other, or you'll have a very peaceful meal. The children will be back here at the church at four o'clock. I'll see you sometime after that, Lili. Have a good day."

She nodded at them and walked quickly away, catching up with Luis, the young hand who worked for Daniel. He saw her coming and waited with a sweet smile. "Can I help you, Miss Rosa?"

"Luis, would you mind taking me to the Blue Moon? Lili needs the car to bring Toby and Susannah home later."

Whatever his plans, Luis politely agreed to drive her home. They chatted about the weather, the rodeo and other minor topics for most of the ride. As they approached the ranch entrance, though, Rosa said what was on her mind.

"I knew a Luis once, a long time ago. Luis Medina."

Luis nodded. "That was my uncle, my mother's brother. I was named after him."

For once, Rosa was speechless. How could she have known that this boy was related to *her* Luis?

But she had known in her heart. "You look much like him," she said, fighting to keep her voice steady.

"That's what they say." Luis glanced in the rearview mirror before taking the turn into the Blue Moon gates. "I've seen a couple of pictures. He got drafted, during that war in the sixties."

"The Vietnam War."

"That's it. And he was missing in action for a while before they finally declared him dead."

"Yes." Rosa fingered the bracelet she never took off, then pulled it down her arm, out from underneath her sleeve. "This has his name on it." She held her hand up to show Luis.

"Really?" He slowed down to look, then glanced at her with a puzzled expression. "How did you know my uncle? I mean, the Medina family isn't on the same level with the Mercados, you know? He was just out of high school when he got drafted."

"He worked for my father, helping with the horses. I loved to ride, then, and I was determined to gentle this wild pinto gelding, who was equally determined not to be ridden. Luis and I worked together that summer." She sighed. "We never did tame the horse. Father sold him to a rodeo, and my Luis went to war."

The young man stopped his car on the driveway in front of the house. "Your Luis? You had a…a thing?"

Rosa smiled at him. "We had a thing. My father was furious, of course, and so we were going to run away. But then…"

"Man." Luis shook his head. "My mom doesn't even know about this. She'll be surprised when I tell her."

"I'd like to hear from her if she wants to call." Opening the door, Rosa got out of the car. "Thank you for the ride, Luis. And for telling me about your uncle."

"Thank you, Miss Rosa. I'll see you again, I hope."

She watched him pull out of the driveway and waved as he headed back toward the gates. A link had been made, connecting past and present. Luis and she had not been able to share children. But he lived on in a new generation.

And for Rosa, that would have to be enough.

WILLA AND DANIEL SPOTTED A CUT through the fence wire just before noon, almost as soon as they crossed onto New Moon land. No effort had been made to disguise the vandalism. Hoofprints indicated that cattle had left the pasture.

Daniel stood for minutes just staring, jaw clenched and hands fisted. Then he dragged himself onto his horse and urged the gelding into a lope, heading toward a distant ridge that overlooked a creek bed where the herd tended to gather.

"I count thirty-five out of fifty," he said, when Willa caught up with him. "Thirty damn percent of the herd stolen."

"You'll have to call the sheriff." She put a hand on his arm. "I'm sorry, Daniel. I feel responsible for your loss."

He shrugged one shoulder. "Your cattle or mine…I'm not sure it makes much difference. But it's got to stop." After a minute, he blew out a long breath. "Want to eat lunch down by the creek?"

"Sure."

They made their way down the hillside at a walk, so as not to spook the cattle, and forded the shallow stream to keep the horses well away from the herd. Willa pointed out a stand of willows with a nice stretch of grass underneath where the horses could graze during the picnic.

A huge, flat-topped boulder right by the creek served as a luncheon table and seating. "The kids and I used to come here a lot." She spread a blue-checked cloth over the rock. "In summer and fall, the banks are gentle and the water's so low that I never worried about them swimming here."

Daniel looked around, trying to get past the rage still pulsing through him. "Peaceful," he agreed. "And safe. I find the herd hanging around here most of the time."

Willa paused in the process of taking food out of the saddle bags. "It's not so safe when the rains come. This dribble can turn torrential in a matter of hours. Further downstream, the sides of the creek get high and the water moves fast." She shook her head. "Sometimes it seems like there are two sides to everything in Texas—and you're never sure whether you'll get the good side or the bad."

"Most of the world is like that, I think. Iraq is largely barren desert, but I saw some really beautiful places there, too."

"Maybe that's just life?"

Daniel thought about the pleasures—and the pain—of the past two months. He'd started building his dream, only to find that it wouldn't be complete without Willa to share it. "Yeah, I think that's just life."

After a quiet lunch, they packed up the empty food containers. Then Willa sat down on the rock beside Daniel. "Do you want to continue checking fence? Or we could go back to your place and call Hobbs Sutton."

"Both, I guess. We can check the fence, and I'll call tonight. There's nothing he can do right now." Putting a hand on her shoulder, he turned her slightly to face him. "Thanks for riding out with me today. I know you have other work to do."

Her cheeks turned a bright red. "I owe you, after waking you up in the middle of the night, sobbing in your ear and then falling asleep on the phone."

"You don't owe me anything, Willa." He skimmed his knuckles along the smooth line of her jaw. "But I'll take whatever you want to give."

Her palm covered the back of his hand. "I think Bev may be right. You are too good to be true." Slipping her fingers through his hair, Willa drew his head down and pressed her lips against his mouth.

Daniel stayed still, eyes closed, and let Willa direct the moment. Each of his remaining senses came sharply to life. He heard the breeze rustling through the leaves above their heads and the grass in the pasture, the trickle of water over rock. The smells of cattle and dirt and water came to him, along with a sweet scent of flowers that belonged to Willa alone.

Most powerfully, he knew the shape of her mouth as she kissed his throat, his jawline, his chin. The firmness of her lips, the press of her fingers against his skull and the nape of his neck—each separate touch stoked the need inside him. Her mouth returned to his, and she bit gently on his lower lip, then slipped the tip of her tongue over the same spot.

He could endure only so much. Closing his arms around her, he pulled her against him and took control with deep, demanding kisses, with his hands on her skin under her shirt, with husky words muttered as they gasped for breath.

"I love you, Willa. Do you know that, yet? God, I love you."

Willa gasped as she heard the words. Caught up in the frenzy of desire, she didn't have the breath to respond, except with her mouth, with her hands and body. Desperate to be closer, she pressed her hips, her breasts, into him. He gave a laugh that was half groan and let her weight send him backward, to lie on the rock.

In the next instant, he started swearing. "Ow-w-w. God, that hurts." His hands gripped her shoulders and pushed her away, not roughly but with unanswerable force. Then he rolled to his stomach, pressing his face against the tablecloth, pounding a fist against the rock beneath. "Damn, damn, damn."

She put a hand on his back. "Are you okay?"

He shook his head and didn't answer. Gradually, the pounding fist slowed, stopped, relaxed. His shoulders loosened and lifted on a deep breath.

"Sorry." He turned his face to the side. His eyes were still squeezed shut. "My back and hip are about as flexible as this boulder."

"It's okay." Now she could breathe, and her pulse had steadied. Her brain was working again. "There are better places for…that kind of thing."

With his hands flat against the rock, Daniel pushed himself backward until his feet touched the ground, then straightened up. He wiped his sleeve across his face and gave her a rueful smile. "'That kind of thing?'"

Willa scooted off the boulder, grabbed up the tablecloth and started folding. "You never know who might be watching."

He made a show of looking around them. "I see your point. We had a whole audience of cows, just for starters."

She couldn't help smiling as she stuffed the cloth into the saddle bag. "Exactly." Then she glanced at him. "Are you ready to go on? Can you ride?"

He took a couple of experimental steps. "I'll be okay." A few more steps brought him to stand right in front of her. Putting a finger under her chin, he tipped her face to his.

"I meant what I said. You don't have to do or say anything right now. Just remember. I love you." He kissed her mouth, quick and hard, then turned to limp stiffly toward the horses.

Willa believed him. And she would remember. But what she wasn't sure of, as they rode through the rest of the beautiful afternoon, was what she wanted—needed—to tell him in return.

JUST BEFORE DINNER THAT NIGHT, Willa opened the front door to find Hobbs Sutton on the veranda. "Good evening, Sheriff. Come in."

He stepped inside and shut the door behind him. "Nice to see you, Willa. How's everything?"

"You mean, except for my son who's still on suspension from school and the rustlers working out of the desert around my ranch?" She grinned at him, then led the way into the parlor. "Great. Just great. Have a seat."

He nodded as he took the chair she indicated. "I just looked at the two fence breaks with Daniel. I'll be filing a report, of course. And I'll put out a notice with auction houses and feed lot managers about the missing cattle. Not that I'll get much cooperation, 'specially on the other side of the border. Short of catching the rustlers red-handed, I don't have much to offer."

"I know. I'm most worried about what Daniel might decide to do on his own."

"Yeah, I could see the wheels spinning in his brain. Unless he keeps a twenty-four-hour watch all along the fence, he doesn't have much recourse. And I don't think he's got enough hands for that kind of operation, does he?"

"No, though I wouldn't put it past him to hire more."

"Deep pockets, I guess." Hobbs leaned forward, bracing his

elbows on his knees. "Listen, Willa, the main reason I stopped by is…" He took a deep breath. "There's a…a good movie coming to Laredo next week, one of those prize-winners everybody talks about. I wondered if you would have dinner with me on the weekend, and see the film. Whatever night works best for you."

Willa couldn't quite hide her surprise. "I—"

The sheriff raised a hand. "You can think about it, let me know later in the week." On his feet again, he looked down at her with a gentle longing in his eyes. "I'd really like to see you more often. You're a special woman, Willa. Special to me."

She dropped her gaze to her own fingers, woven tightly together in her lap. After a few seconds, she realized what she had to say. Getting to her feet, she stepped forward and took his hands in hers.

"Hobbs, I really appreciate your invitation. I like you, and I know you're a good man."

His face changed. "But?"

"But I don't want to lead you on. I'll always be your friend, but that's all I'll ever be."

"It's been two years, darlin'. You don't have to mourn forever."

"I won't." Willa took a deep breath. Was she ready to say this? "There's someone…someone else."

After a long silence, he said, "Daniel."

She nodded. "I don't know what will happen. But—"

"It's okay. I understand." Hobbs stepped back, out of her reach, and stared at her for a moment, then turned and went toward the entry hall. "Let me know if you get anymore rustling out this way. I'll see what I can do to muster up additional help." Opening the door, he stepped outside without looking at her again. "'Bye, Willa. Good luck."

"Goodbye, Hobbs."

The thud of the door against its frame sounded permanent. Final. One part of her life ended, another just beginning.

As she walked toward the kitchen, she came face-to-face

with Robbie in the hallway. He carried a bowl of ice cream in one hand and an entire package of chocolate cream–filled cookies in the other.

"Health food," she said, trying for a joke.

Rolling his eyes, he brushed by her. "Whatever."

She whirled and caught his arm. "Roberto, I am your mother and you'll treat me with respect. You know that is the very least your father would demand."

At the mention of his father, Robbie's shoulders slumped. "Yes, ma'am."

Willa released him. "Thank you."

"Can I go now?"

"Yes."

The slam of his bedroom door told her all she needed to know about her older son's state of mind.

As they cleaned up the kitchen after dinner, Rosa shared with Lili what she had learned during her ride home with Luis. Then she waited for her sister to volunteer an account of her afternoon with Nate Hernandez.

But when the counters had been wiped, the dishwasher started and the light turned off, Lili hadn't said a word. As they folded the latest load of laundry from the dryer, Rosa couldn't contain her curiosity any longer.

"Did you enjoy your afternoon?"

Lili carefully smoothed imaginary wrinkles from a pillow-case. "Oh, yes." Her cheeks turned a delicate shade of rose.

"Where did you go for lunch?"

"Um, The Trellis."

"My goodness, that's a very fancy restaurant."

"It was nice."

When she didn't say more, Rosa sighed in frustration. "What did you talk about?"

Lili jumped, as if startled out of a dream. "Um, things. About the children, and Willa and Daniel. About Jamie, a little. About when Nate worked here." She smiled. "We used to talk while he worked in the barn. I would bring him lunch, out in the farthest pastures, when he rode the fence line."

"I remember." Rosa nodded. "Where did you go after lunch?" When Lili looked puzzled, she clarified. "Yesterday."

"Oh." She finished another pillowcase before answering. "We walked around the historic part of Laredo. Then we went back to the church, the youth group arrived, and I brought the children home."

"Did he kiss you?" Lili looked up, eyes wide, mouth an *O* of surprise. Rosa gave a smile of satisfaction. "That's good. Did you make plans for another date?"

"He didn't ask."

"Did you ask him?"

"How could I do that?"

Rosa grabbed up a stack of towels for Willa's bathroom. "You say, 'Nate, come for dinner Wednesday night.' Or, 'Nate, I'd like to see a movie next weekend. Will you go with me?'" She glared at her sister. "I wash my hands of the two of you. If you can't think for yourselves any better than this, you really don't deserve your own happiness."

She ran into Willa in the hallway and shoved the towels into her arms with a mumbled "Good night." Then Rosa went to her bedroom, curled up on her bed with her bracelet next to her heart and shed bitter tears—for her sister, and for herself.

AFTER THREE WEEKS OF ROB'S silent, unquestioning labor, Daniel decided to precipitate a reaction—rage, sorrow, defiance, he didn't care. The kid needed to talk…or yell. Maybe that would be easier with somebody he hated.

On Tuesday, he sent Nate with the hands to check the herds

and kept Rob with him to work on the old storeroom in the barn, which he was turning into an office. Under Nate's supervision, Rob had carried out grimy tins, tubs, boxes and buckets. Today, they would rip off the rough boards nailed up as makeshift shelving, then wash down the ceiling, walls and floor.

"After that," Daniel told Rob as they began prying the first board, "the room will be fit for human habitation."

Rob applied leverage to his hammer but didn't say a word.

"You go back to school next week?"

No answer.

"You'll have to do some hard work to make up for the failing grades, I guess."

A nail screamed as it tore loose, but Rob didn't reply.

The gradual approach wasn't working. Daniel aimed straight for the heart. "Do you think your dad would be proud of what you've done?"

Rob threw him a furious glance. "None of your business."

"Was he the kind of man to lie and steal and cheat?"

Finally, the boy faced him. "You know he wasn't. He was a soldier. He did the right thing."

"Maybe the real reason you're so mad is because he left in the first place. If he'd cared about you, and your mom and Toby and Susannah, he would have stayed home. But he left, because you weren't—"

"Shut up! Shut up, shut up!" Rob came at him, both arms swinging. He butted his head into Daniel's belly, punching and kicking. "He cared about us, he cared about his country. You shut up!"

He landed some solid hits before Daniel got hold of his arms and forced them wide apart. His fury far from spent, Rob kept trying to kick, aiming at Daniel's bad leg.

"That's enough." Daniel grunted at a direct slam to his knee. He shook the boy hard. "That is enough!"

Rob stood still, glaring and panting. "Take it back. Take what you said back."

"I take it back. I believe your dad loved his family very much." Daniel released his grip. "The question is, do you?"

For a long moment, Rob didn't speak, didn't move. Then his hands clenched, unclenched. He spun around, and Daniel thought he would take off out the door.

Instead, he dove to pick up the hammer he'd dropped.

Daniel held up both hands. "Rob…" For a second, he feared for his life.

But Rob laid into wood instead of flesh. He pounded the shelf he'd been working on and the wall behind it, over and over, as fast as he could draw back his arm.

There were words between the blows. "Why? Why didn't *you* die? Why couldn't *he* be the one who came back?" Tears streaked through the dirt on his face. "Why did he have to go there, anyway? We wanted him here. I needed him here."

Daniel closed his eyes, hearing the echo of Willa's words.

"I hate him for going." Rob spoke softly, then louder. "I hate him for leaving us! I hate him. I hate him." He stopped hammering and stared at Daniel, across the room. "I hate you!"

The hammer flew into the corner farthest from where Daniel stood. As it landed, the boy broke for the door. Through the window, Daniel saw him race across the ground, heading toward home.

Nate came in a short while later and took stock of the room's condition. "What's happened here?"

"A hurricane," Daniel told him. "Here's hoping it cleared the air."

Chapter Thirteen

Some advantages of a military background were the skills you developed and the contacts you came away with—like the friend specializing in counter-terrorism technology who was currently on leave at home in Dallas. After several phone consultations and a drive to the Big *D*, Daniel had assembled the equipment he required to deal with the enemy stealing his cattle. Three fourteen-hour days of work got the system up and running. With Nate's help, he set up a command center in the barn, complete with receivers for the signals from sensors on the fence lines, a phone connection and satellite computer hookup. Now he would know when his fences were cut and he could catch the bastards in the act.

He didn't mention the plan to Willa, because she would want the sheriff's department involved or else veto the whole enterprise. Daniel planned to call the sheriff when the system alerted him that the rustlers were operational. Otherwise, Sutton would simply say he didn't have the personnel to sit on their butts and wait for an alarm.

The week of Thanksgiving brought rain—hours of downpour every day. Daniel, Nate and the hands kept watch in the pastures for cows in trouble—stuck in the mud, stranded on the wrong side of a rushing creek, struck by branches from windblown trees. Daniel came in every day wet and exhausted to fall asleep in the barn with the console monitoring his fences, then started over again the next morning at dawn.

Though his crew argued with him, he gave them all Thanksgiving Day off. He and Nate could handle any emergency in the fields. Maybe the storms would break for the holiday.

No such luck. He woke on Thursday morning to the same old sound of rain pounding on the roof, plus the ringing of the telephone.

"Boss…"

He barely recognized the weak voice. "Nate?"

"Boss, I cain't get there this morning. I cain't move three feet away from the john."

"That's bad. Something you ate?"

"Maybe. Got a couple of burritos on the way home last night. Woke up a few hours later with my guts twisted like barb wire." He made a choking sound. "Gotta go."

Daniel hung up the phone and lay back with a groan. No problem. He could take care of his ranch by himself. He hoped.

His invitation for dinner with Willa and her family was for five. If he started early and ate in the saddle, he could check on all the pastures and be home with enough time to clean up.

He began with the herd farthest from the house, grateful that he didn't have to check the fence line as well as search out cows in danger. By the time he stopped for lunch at noon, he felt pretty confident. All the cattle had been present and accounted for, with no imminent threats he could see. Even the rain had backed off to a sporadic sprinkle.

Then he reached the field where he and Willa had picnicked by the creek. The wind picked up and the sky darkened, with the rain beginning again in earnest. He counted thirty cows, where there should have been thirty-five, thanks to the rustlers. After two recounts, he was certain—more cattle were missing.

Daniel sat there on his horse in the pouring rain, wondering what a seasoned, experienced rancher would do. Of all the times for Nate to be sick…

Wiping his face with a hand gloved in wet leather, he stared at the ground around him, hoping for some indication of what course to follow. Four days of rain had turned the soil to liquid mud in which hoofprints melted away after a few minutes. The creek had risen several feet up the gentle slope of its banks, a churning brown soup of foam, rocks and tree limbs. He thought about how pretty the place had been just a couple of weeks ago, when he'd kissed Willa on the rock and told her he loved her. That day, he'd begun to believe he could have his dream ranch *and* the woman he needed.

Something else from that day jingled a bell in his mind. Chasing down the memory, he remembered her explanation of how dangerous the little stream could be when the rains came. Like now.

Following the direction she'd indicated that day, he rode farther north along the path of the creek, allowing Calypso to pick his way slowly across the slippery ground. Just as Willa had said, the banks became steeper the farther he went, and the water moved faster. What cow would be stupid enough to get caught up in this surging, roaring flood?

Even as he asked himself the question, he heard a pitiful call from somewhere up ahead. Calypso pricked his ears and moved toward the sound without prompting. They came to a cluster of willows and shrubs growing beside the creek, and Daniel discovered a path he hadn't seen before, a depression worn into the sides of the ravine that took the cattle directly to the creek bed itself. The U-shaped tunnel was already half-filled with muddy water.

And on the other bank, where a similar chute led down to the creek, three of his missing cows stood lined up as if to come back across.

Cursing the stupidity of cattle and the lack of cell phone transmitters, Daniel rode Calypso as fast as he dared across the five miles back to his barn.

In keeping with today's luck, however, Rob answered the phone at the Mercado house. "She's...uh...not here."

Daniel forced himself to stay calm. "I'll try the barn."

"Not there, either. She went into town."

"Right. On Thanksgiving Day, when all the stores are closed, your mother drove into town in the pouring rain. Give me a break. Just put her on the phone, please."

"I told you, she's not here."

"Look, son—"

"I'm not your son."

"And right now you should be thanking God for that fact." He pulled in a deep breath. "Look, Rob, I've got animals in trouble and nobody to ask for help but your mother. If I have to ride down to your house, I will, but the more time I waste, the more likely it is those stupid cows will die. Do you want that to happen?"

He held his breath through a silence that seemed to last forever.

Finally, Rob said, "Mom? Phone." Then came a crash that sounded like the phone itself landing on a tile floor, followed by a long silence. Was there still a connection?

And then Willa said, "Hello?"

Daniel closed his eyes in relief. "Thank God. I need your help, Willa. Can you come?"

She arrived at his barn fifteen minutes after he'd finished his explanation, carrying an insulated container of coffee. "Lili and Rosa insisted I make you drink a cup before we leave. If you've been out all day, you need to warm up." A glance over his shoulder took in the equipment he'd installed. "This is pretty fancy. What's going on?"

"I'll explain later. I rubbed Calypso down and gave him some water. Do you think he can go out again?"

She surveyed the horse as he stood munching hay in one of the stalls. "He's good and strong. He'll be fine." Her gaze came back to Daniel. "I'm more worried about you. You're worn to the bone."

"I'm okay. Let's just get out there and do something about those cows."

On the trip back across the range, Daniel realized he was riding on instinct, his body numbed by exhaustion and beyond his conscious control. He'd be depending on Willa's strength for whatever rescue his animals required.

Back at the creek, Daniel reined in Calypso with a groan of dismay. Only two cows now stood on the opposite bank.

He shouted to Willa above the wind and rain. "Do you think one of them could have climbed back out?"

She gave him a long look that expressed her doubts. "Let's see about getting these two back to the herd."

Expecting her to use the ropes she'd brought along to pull the cows across, he was surprised when Willa headed Monty downstream, toward the shallower part of the creek. Calypso followed without encouragement or direction from his rider, and Daniel began to realize how useless he'd become in this situation.

They found the first carcass about a quarter of a mile along, lodged against the trunk of a willow tree standing in the path of the flood. A second cow lay a few yards further. Both had been pregnant. Daniel used every ounce of will he possessed to swallow down the gorge that rose in his throat.

When Willa reached the relatively shallow section of the creek, she turned her horse and waited for Daniel to catch up. "The horses can ford here. We'll go get those cows—drag them up the bank backward, if we have to—and drive them back to where they can cross and join the herd." She put a hand on his arm. "I'm sorry about those two back there."

"If I'd known what to do…"

"The outcome wouldn't have changed. You lose cattle, Daniel, no matter how long you've been ranching. Don't blame yourself."

"Sure." He straightened up. "So, let's do what we can."

Willa headed Monty into the fast-moving creek, which rose quickly to hit her above the knee. The current pushed the horse sideways, and Monty snorted as foam and spray hit his face, but Willa kept him moving forward, across the flow. This time, Calypso balked at following until Daniel finally flicked the ends of the reins over Cal's hip to make his point. Snorting, Cal stepped gingerly off the muddy bank.

The force of the cold water was terrifying. The sensation of sinking, with a horse under him, threatened to paralyze Daniel. He couldn't think, couldn't move. If he got across safely, Calypso could claim all the credit.

Slowly—too slowly—they made their way across the twenty feet of water now comprising the creek. Willa waited on the other side. "You've got it made," she yelled. "Just a few more steps."

At that moment, Cal stumbled, pitching forward. His head went under the water. Daniel felt the horse roll to the right… toward his bad leg, the one he couldn't slip out of the stirrup in a hurry. He knew he was going under and grabbed a breath of air.

The water closed over his head, filling ears and eyes and nose with silt. Beside him, Calypso thrashed, trying to find his feet. Daniel wondered if he'd get kicked before he could free his right foot. Or would the horse drag him out of the water foot-first?

With a mighty surge, Cal leapt through the water, and Daniel fell free. He hit bottom, rolled along the gravel-crusted creek bed and then came to rest sitting up, with the surface of the water just above his head. Using arms and legs that felt like logs, he pushed himself up…up…into the air. And the steadily falling rain.

"Damn rain," he muttered, trying to wipe the mud out of his eyes so he could see. "I hate the damn rain."

"Are you okay?" Willa's voice came from somewhere nearby. When he could finally open his eyes, she was just above him on the bank, with the reins of both horses in one hand and the other held out to him. "Get out of the water, cowboy."

"Yeah, right." He wasn't sure he could move. His leg and his back had gone from cold and numb to searing pain. Waving her hand away, he bent his good knee and struggled to his feet on his own. "I've got it. I'm okay."

The first step he took made him realize that somewhere in the process of nearly drowning he'd lost his right boot.

"Still in the stirrup," Willa told him, when she saw him stop mid-stride. "Cal saved it for you."

Daniel was beyond comment. Weary and aching, he floundered out of the creek, pulled his boot out of the stirrup and shoved his foot inside. Then, using their lunch table rock to mount, he struggled back into the saddle. "Let's get the cows. I'm ready to quit for the day." Or maybe longer.

The prodigal cows had, of their own accord, moved away from the water and back onto solid ground, so the process of getting them back to the herd became relatively simple. Even crossing back across the creek posed few problems this time, and the two animals trotted back to join the herd with bovine nonchalance. Of the fifth animal there was no sign, alive or dead.

"I'll send a couple of hands out to look tomorrow," Daniel said. "Maybe she was smarter than the rest." Which was more than could be said for the man who ran the ranch.

It was after four o'clock by the time he and Willa made it back to his barn. "Don't stop here," he told her. "Go straight to your place, take care of the horse and get yourself warm and dry. I'll take a shower and be there for dinner at five, as invited." He tried out a grin for her benefit.

Judging by her worried gaze, his effort wasn't much of a success. "You're not taking this well."

He made his usual clumsy exit from the saddle, avoiding Willa's eyes by working on loosening the wet girth around Cal's belly. "I'll be fine once I get dry. Go on, now. See you in a little while." Not waiting for her to leave, he turned and led his horse into the barn, to food and water and a rubdown with several dry towels.

When he walked into the kitchen of his house half an hour later, Trouble commenced his standard greeting routine—yips and yaps, excessive panting and tongue lolling, circles run clockwise and counter-clockwise around Daniel's feet and, finally, a running leap that plowed his front paws square into the belly. When he regained his breath, Daniel clipped a leash onto the dog's collar and went back out into the rain to take care of canine business. He'd been thinking about putting up a fence at the back of the house so Trouble could have room to run and wouldn't have to be on a leash, for his own protection and that of the cattle. Maybe it was a good thing he hadn't yet gotten around to spending that particular chunk of cash.

In the house once more, he gave the dog his dinner and finally took off his soaked duster and soggy boots, hanging them to drip in a sheltered corner of the carport. In the bathroom, he peeled away layers of drenched clothing to find his skin puckered and pale…where it wasn't purple and red with scars, of course. His whole body shook, with exhaustion, probably, coupled with reaction and maybe a touch of hypothermia. He turned the hot water on as far as it would go, adding just enough cold to keep from burning himself. Propping his hands on the tiles, Daniel stood under the shower spray and gave himself permission to stop thinking.

WILLA WASN'T SURPRISED WHEN Daniel didn't appear promptly at five o'clock. She'd told Lili and Rosa that he would probably be late, because he needed some time to clean up and recover before he came down to dinner. They'd agreed to postpone the final whipping of the mashed potatoes and the carving of the turkey until five-thirty.

But Daniel hadn't arrived by five-thirty.

"When are we gonna eat?" Toby leaned against the kitchen counter, rubbing his stomach and looking pitiful. "I'm starved."

"We're waiting for Major Trent." Willa ruffled his hair as she walked by. "He should be here any second."

She continued on to her bedroom, where she sat down on the bed, picked up the phone and dialed the number she now knew by heart. After six rings, she heard the clatter of the handset being fumbled, and a curse, which she took to mean he'd answered the call.

"Daniel? It's Willa."

After a long time, he said, "Hi." His voice sounded like a tape recording played at extra slow speed.

"Are you asleep, Daniel?"

"Uh…yeah. I think so."

Willa smiled. "See you later, then. Sleep well."

"Sure." This pause lasted so long, she started to hang up, when she heard him say, "Thanks, Willa. 'Preciate it."

"Any time," she said softly.

Although the meal was delicious, as always, only Robbie truly enjoyed Thanksgiving dinner that evening. The rest of the family had been looking forward to having Daniel join them.

Lili sighed, gazing at the end of the table where Daniel's place remained empty. "He's been here so often for dinner in the last few weeks, the table doesn't seem quite right without him."

"We made extra potatoes and dressing, because he always enjoys his food." Rosa shook her head. "And he needs fattening up. He's working too hard and losing weight."

Willa winced from the memory of watching Daniel go underwater in the creek that afternoon. "He is working too hard. Maybe I'll suggest he needs to hire a couple of extra hands."

"We could take him some dinner," Susannah suggested. "And keep him company while he ate. That would be like having a second Thanksgiving dinner!"

"Oh, wow," Robbie said sarcastically. "Wouldn't that be fun?"

"You're a jerk," his sister replied. "You don't have to come."

"I wouldn't come if you asked."

"So who's asking?" Toby stuck out his tongue at his brother. "Nobody wants you around, anyway."

"That's enough." Willa used the voice that never failed to restore order. "All three of you are behaving badly, especially for Thanksgiving dinner. Say something nice, or you can go to your room without dessert."

The rest of the meal passed in almost total silence.

During cleanup, though, Rosa said, "I think you should take Daniel some dinner, Willa. If he fell asleep, he hasn't had anything to eat all afternoon."

"And he probably didn't eat much breakfast or lunch." Lili took down a set of plastic containers.

"I don't want to wake him up to eat." Willa felt obligated to protest. But she welcomed the excuse to check on Daniel. What she'd seen in his face this afternoon, as he'd absorbed the loss of a few animals, needed to be dealt with.

Rosa quickly brushed off that token objection. "He'll rest better if he's eaten." Bringing out a basket, she packed the containers Lili had filled, added a jug of lemonade and a whole pumpkin pie, plus a spray can of whipped cream. "Not as good as homemade but better than nothing."

Toby and Susannah came into the kitchen as Willa was shrugging into her raincoat. "We're ready to go," Toby announced. "I'm bringing Trouble a new sock as his Thanksgiving present."

Susannah peeked into the basket. "And I helped make the pies, so I'm bringing something, too."

Willa gazed at her son and daughter, half-inclined to take the easy way out and take them along. Daniel enjoyed the kids, and their presence would ensure a nice, safe, casual evening….

Rosa stepped forward and put a hand on the children's shoulders. "I think—"

"You're both really sweet," Willa said. "But I think Daniel's had enough excitement for one day, and three visitors might just be too many to handle." Their faces fell, and she felt a surge of guilt. "I'm going to take the food, warm it up for him, maybe talk to him a little while he eats. Then he's probably going to go straight back to—to sleep. You two can visit tomorrow, or Saturday, when he's had some rest."

They still didn't look too happy. "Besides, you wanted to watch the movie at eight tonight. And it's almost that now. Give me a kiss, because I might get back after you go to bed."

She leaned down for a hug from each of them and then shooed them out of the kitchen. Lili handed her the basket of food, and Rosa held out the keys to the truck.

"We won't be waiting up," she said, with a wink. "But I'd try to be back before breakfast, if I were you."

Willa stared at her aunt-in-law. "I—I—"

"Just go." Lili gave her a slight push toward the back door. "Now."

WILLA'S WARM HAND against his cheek, Willa's soft lips pressing a kiss on his forehead. Willa's soft voice next to his ear. "Wake up, cowboy. You need to eat."

"Mmm." Without opening his eyes, Daniel stretched out an arm and found that he could arch it naturally around Willa's waist. "Maybe." Shaping his hand over her hip, he pulled her over to lean against him. "What's on the menu?"

He heard Willa's deep breath. "Whatever you're hungry for."

Daniel opened his eyes then, and found her gazing at him with a mixture of nerves and laughter and desire in her face. Shifting his other arm out from underneath him, he took her hand in his. "You, Willa. Only you."

When he tugged that hand, she bent toward him, and her rich black hair fell loosely around his head and shoulders. With a twist of her hips, she straightened her legs out along the length of his and lay down next to him, knee-to-knee, hip-to-hip, face-to-face.

"Nice," Daniel whispered, running a hand along the slope of her back, from shoulder to thigh. "You fit like you belong here."

She smiled at him, a full-fledged, nothing-held-back curve of those wide, sweet lips. "Maybe I do. Make love to me, Daniel. Please?"

He grinned, acknowledging the fact that she'd asked and what that meant for them both. "My pleasure."

She'd worn a loose shirt, easy to draw over her head. Underneath, she was slim and smooth, sexy as hell in a lacy white bra. He traced the edge of her rib cage with his thumb, testing the border of that bra with his fingertips. "Café au lait," he whispered across her collarbone. "With lots of sugar."

Willa bowed her spine, bringing the swell of her breast to his attention. "Daniel . . ."

"Yes, ma'am." His rough skin snagged the strap at her shoulder as he slid it down her arm. A lace cup sagged, and Willa's breast slipped free. The perfume she wore surrounded him, like a room full of flowers. He dragged in a deep breath.

And then he claimed his own.

Chapter Fourteen

They made it into the kitchen at midnight. Willa put the micro-wave to good use, and they shared Thanksgiving dinner at the kitchen table with Trouble watching every bite they took.

"This was delicious." Daniel finished the last of his second piece of pumpkin pie and sat back with a groan. "You're a great cook."

"You know that's not true. You saw the extent of my culinary skills tonight—microwave magic. Lili and Rosa have been the only kitchen talents at the Blue Moon since Jamie was born, at least. I never even tried to learn."

"Why would you? You've got other skills and important work to do." He set their plates on the floor for Toby to lick clean and put the rest of the dishware in the sink. "My specialty is cleaning up."

"A truly vital contribution." She glanced at the clock on the stove and sighed. "I should go home."

He pulled her to her feet and closed his arms around her. "You could stay a few more hours. The kids are asleep by now."

She rested her head on the hollow in his shoulder made for that purpose. "I'd rather not sneak in at dawn." Looking up at him, she grinned. "I'll just have to bring you another meal sometime soon."

"Sounds good." He kissed her, celebrating the freedom to do so, the luxury of being able to relax and simply enjoy touching the woman he loved. "I'll walk you to your truck."

Outside, a dry wind had started pushing the storm toward the eastern coast. Stars peeked out occasionally, only to be hidden again by the next patch of clouds.

"Now the rain stops." Daniel blew a frustrated breath as he thought, yet again, about the day's disasters.

Willa rubbed a hand up and down his arm. "You'll recover, Daniel. You have to, if you're going to survive in the cattle business."

That's just the point. Maybe I won't survive. Not a possibility he wanted to share with her tonight.

Before he could think of what to say instead, she glanced in the direction of the barn. He followed her gaze, thinking she'd seen something unusual, then realized what had caught her attention—the green glow of monitor buttons and screens through the window of the office.

Willa looked back at him. "What is all that high-tech stuff? You didn't get a chance to explain earlier."

He cleared his throat. "I set up a monitoring system on my fences."

"What kind of system? Motion detectors? Wouldn't that catch any kind of activity—like a lizard crossing the fence line?"

"Right." He ran a hand over his face. "This system doesn't detect motion. It senses when the fence line has been broken. Or cut."

Her eyes narrowed as she thought through what he'd said. "In other words, you've set it up to warn you when the rustlers cut the fence. You plan to sneak up on them while they're in the middle of stealing cattle."

"Yeah."

Hands on her hips, she faced him. "Don't you want to correct me on that? Don't you want to tell me that your plan is to call Hobbs Sutton so *he and his deputies* can sneak up and catch the rustlers before they get away?"

"I will call the sheriff as soon as I get an alarm. But, Willa, you know how long it would take them to come this far out from town. That's part of the problem. Sutton can't post deputies indefinitely, but the only way to catch these thieves is to have someone right here, ready to spring the trap." Daniel shrugged. "That someone has got to be me."

"You and Nate? You and at least one other hand? Do you know how dangerous those men are?"

"This isn't Nate's ranch. The hands don't have twenty-four/seven responsibility. And most of them have families, people who care about them. I can't ask them to risk their lives."

"You'll just risk your own." He'd never heard such deadly cold in her voice, not even that very first day. "And to top it all off, you weren't going to tell me, were you? You figured you'd just show up at breakfast one morning and announce it? 'Oh, by the way, I had this neat gadget installed and I caught all the rustlers single-handed last night. Don't have a scratch on me and they're all in jail.' Something like that?"

"Something like that."

"Damn it, Daniel!" She walked an agitated circle in front of him, then stopped to glare at him again. "You're going to do whatever *you* think is best, without consulting me, without giving me a chance to express my opinion or change your mind."

"I do depend on you, Willa. I couldn't have gotten through this afternoon without you. But—"

"I could help with this, you know. I'm a damn good shot."

"You've got three children who depend on *you* to take care of them."

"You made *me* depend on *you!* You led me to believe I could trust you to be here, that I would be safe being with you. And all the time you're setting up this plot that's more than likely going to get you killed and leave me grieving again."

"Willa—"

He reached for her, but she brushed him off. "You do whatever you have to—though I can assure you, no piece of beef is worth the kind of risk you're prepared to take. But stay away from me, and stay away from my family. We've been hurt enough. Just go your own way, and we'll go ours."

She jumped into her truck, spraying gravel as she turned around and headed down the hill toward the Blue Moon.

Daniel stood for a long time staring blindly into the darkness. Then he went back into his house, got dressed and spent the rest of the night monitoring his fences from the barn.

NATE ARRIVED FRIDAY MORNING looking pale but steady on his feet. Daniel sent him with three of the hands out to pick up the dead cattle. The first truck got stuck in the mud, as did the second he sent to the rescue. Finally, Nate drove down to Willa's barn to ask for the loan of a tractor, which pulled the two trucks back to solid ground and dug a hole big enough to bury the two dead cows.

After such a pleasant morning, Daniel wasn't surprised to see a sheriff's office vehicle coming up the road in the middle of the afternoon.

He invited the sheriff into the house and handed over a glass of lemonade. "Although I suppose you'd rather go to the barn. I gather Willa called you to report on my monitoring system."

Sutton emptied the glass in three gulps. "Thanks. Yeah, she called. I told her what you're doing isn't against the law as far as I can tell. But I think going after the rustlers on your own is a lousy idea."

Daniel set his glass on the counter. "But it's not illegal."

"No. If you shoot or kill somebody, though, I'll probably have to arrest you. And the courts can be tricky about self-defense."

"This is Texas. Don't I have a right to defend my own property?"

Holding up his hands in a gesture of surrender, the sheriff shook his head. "Ask a lawyer. I'm just telling you what's been my experience."

"Thanks for the warning."

"You be sure you call if you go after them. I'll arrive in time to pick up the pieces, at least."

Daniel grinned. "That makes me feel better."

His monitoring system sounded the alert for the first time on the night of December first. Daniel was alone in the barn, dozing in the chair, when the warning lights started flashing and the buzzer sounded. He jerked awake and nearly fell off the chair before he realized what was going on. A quick look at the diagram on the computer screen showed him the segment of fence being attacked. Grabbing his coat and his holster, Daniel headed for his truck. Tonight, he'd get this problem taken care of once and for all.

Then, maybe, he could see about getting Willa to forgive him.

True to his word, he called the sheriff's office before he left the barn, to report the theft. Then he drove twenty minutes across the ranch, avoiding huddles of sleeping cattle, getting in and out of the truck for three separate gates. With a quarter of a mile to go, he parked the truck and started out on foot, hoping to avoid any advance warning to the rustlers.

But as he crested the hill that would give him a good view of the fence, Daniel stopped in his tracks. The moon shone like a spotlight in the clear night sky, defining every shape with sharp black lines and illuminating any movement on the landscape.

He didn't see a single cow between himself and the fence line. No cattle trailer, no ATVs herding animals in that direction. A quiet night on the range stretched to the horizon on every side.

The fence line definitely had been cut—he found the broken wire with ease in the bright light. But when he examined the ground, he felt sure that none of his cattle had been close to this part of the fence since the Thanksgiving rains. On the outside of the fence, he found no tracks at all. Were the rustlers taunting him?

Or had somebody else decided to play games?

THE ARGUMENT BEGAN ON DECEMBER second, as the children brought the boxes holding *el nacimiento*—the Mercado family's elaborate nativity scene—down from the second floor storage room.

"You must ask Daniel to the party," Rosa said in a quiet voice. "How will it look to invite practically the entire county and leave out your closest neighbor?"

Willa handed her one of the vases that usually sat on the table under Jamie's picture and picked up the other one herself. "I don't care how it looks. Let's take these to the kitchen."

When she returned, Lili was spreading a gold brocade cloth over the table. "Nate will be coming." She smoothed an imaginary wrinkle. "And all of Daniel's hands are related to ours in some way or the other. They'll be here. How can we not have Daniel at the *posada,* too?"

Willa waited until the children had gone back upstairs for the rest of the boxes. Then she faced her aunts. "Let me make this very clear. I explained what he's done and told you why I can't trust him. I will not put my children or myself through more of the kind of pain we've endured these past two years. That means I can't have anything to do with Daniel Trent. You may have your *posada* with Toby, Susannah, Roberto and me in the house…or him. That's the only choice."

She thought the decision should be fairly easy. But over the course of the afternoon, as the family set out the elaborate hand-built stand, the antique figurines and accessories that had been collected over generations, Rosa and Lili continued to make pointed comments.

"You would think he was Lucifer himself." Rosa sniffed as she placed the traditional figure of the devil in his dark cave on the back corner of the table.

"The holiday is about love," Lili said simply, as she arranged the angels on the upper levels of the display.

This was Toby's year to place the oldest and most important pieces on the display—the manger holding the Holy Child, and José and Maria, his parents. When he'd finished, he looked over his shoulder at Willa, his brown eyes solemn. "Didn't He tell us to forgive?"

Willa heard Robbie snort. She ignored her older son, and put a hand on Toby's shoulder. "Yes, He did. But we can forgive someone who hurts us without giving them the opportunity to do so again."

That comment earned sounds of frustration from both aunts and from Susannah.

"I don't care what you think," Willa told the three of them. "Lili, Rosa, if you want to see him that's your prerogative. As long as it's not on Blue Moon land. Don't bring him here. And Susannah and Toby will not be going there." She knew she didn't have to tell Robbie. "Is that understood?" The children nodded. The aunts looked mulish.

"Good. Now, what about those tamales I can smell cooking in the kitchen?"

For the next two weeks, they prepared for the party—the aunts always insisted on making all the food themselves while Willa and the children got the house ready. The tradition of the *posada* recalled the journey of José and Maria to Bethlehem, searching for a place in which the Holy Child could be born. The Mercados had been hosting a *posada* at the Blue Moon for at least a century…even the year after Jamie's death, they'd held a quieter version of the annual event. This year, Willa had hoped to enjoy herself thoroughly, dancing and singing the festive songs of the season and introducing Daniel to her family's customs.

Instead, she would be alone. Again.

On Saturday the fourteenth, the day of the party, she and the kids strung lights in the trees around the house and along the top of the courtyard wall. In the courtyard itself, Toby and Robbie hung piñatas—hollow papier-mâché donkeys filled with candy and small presents—at a variety of heights for children of different ages to bat with a stick until the piñata broke open and treats scattered all around. Susannah set candles and pots of brilliant-red poinsettias on the small tables arranged around the fountain. Willa made sure there were plenty of adult refreshments and that her aunts stopped cooking long enough to don their party dresses.

At six, the family gathered in the courtyard as they always did for the official "lighting ceremony." Toby and Robbie plugged in the extension cords for the electric lights, while Susannah, Lili, Willa and Rosa lit the candles. Then they all stepped back to admire the effect. Susannah gasped in pleasure.

Toby pumped his fist in the air. "Awesome!"

"Pretty cool," was Robbie's assessment.

"Beautiful!" Rosa clapped her hands. "This is the prettiest I think I've ever seen it."

Lili dabbed at her eyes. "Father would have been proud." She slipped an arm around Willa's waist. "Jamie, too."

Willa nodded. "It looks wonderful." She turned to hug her aunts and then her kids. "You've all done a terrific job. Now let's enjoy the party!"

The guests would start arriving any minute. Her family scattered to their final tasks, leaving her in the cool evening air by herself for a moment. Reluctantly, she looked north, up the road, as if she could see Daniel's house, two miles away. What was he doing tonight? Had he put her out of his mind? Why couldn't she do the same?

Out beyond the courtyard wall, a car door slammed and then another. With a heavy heart, Willa turned to greet her friends. Maybe she couldn't have a good time, but she would make sure that everyone else did.

AS HE SAT IN HIS BARN OFFICE ON Saturday night, Daniel could have sworn he heard music and laughter coming up the hill from the Blue Moon ranch. Not really, of course. Those sounds wouldn't carry this distance. But he could imagine the house all decked out for the party—a *posada,* Nate said they called it. Daniel could imagine Willa in that blue dress she'd worn to the Cattlemen's Ball, with her hair pinned up and her eyes shining brightly as she danced and enjoyed herself.

And here he was, holed up alone in his one-man crusade to…what? Protect his property? Secure justice?

Or was he hoping to prove—to Willa, to himself—that he was equal to the role he'd taken on?

For that, he would need the cooperation of the rustlers. They would need to show up, cut through his fence and steal his cattle so he could catch them in the act. But in the weeks since he'd installed his system, his cattle had stayed where they belonged, which was a victory, of sorts. Except for the false alarms.

Three times in the past two weeks, his fence had been cut. The alarm had sounded and he'd headed out to the site…only to come up short. No cattle missing, no evidence of rustling. He was beginning to feel like a character in a children's story—*The Boy Who Cried Wolf.* After Hobbs Sutton had shown up the first two times but the rustlers hadn't, Daniel had stopped calling. No man liked being shown for a fool in front of his romantic rival.

He had a feeling Rob Mercado was sneaking out at night to

torment him. He could probably have proved it if he tried. But the tricks were relatively harmless, although they cost him extra work and some lost sleep. Mostly, he didn't want to cause Willa more trouble. The boy would get tired of the game when no one reacted.

Which was why, when the alarm went off at midnight, Daniel considered ignoring it. What better cover for a Saturday night prank than the big party going on at the Blue Moon? Rob would figure that his mother wouldn't miss him with so many people in the house. He could slip out to the barn, saddle Tar and ride off without being seen, then ease back into the crowd an hour later with no one the wiser. Including Daniel.

Then again, maybe this was the rustlers' golden opportunity. Maybe they figured Daniel was at the party, and they had all night to load cattle and take them away. Maybe they'd be a little careless, thinking they couldn't get caught.

Prepared for rustlers but expecting another false alarm, Daniel decided to ride Calypso to check out the fence rather than take the truck. The monitor showed the fence break in the pasture closest to the barn, so they'd have an easy trip out. Another bright moon would keep them both safe.

Fifteen minutes later, as he watched men in black clothes use ATVs to drive his cattle toward a hole in the fence, Daniel discarded all thoughts of safety. He counted three of them doing the herding. Add maybe two more at the truck. The odds weren't great, but he'd succeeded against worse.

About to kick Calypso into action, Daniel realized that he could get plenty of help at Willa's tonight—Nate and his hands, probably Hobbs Sutton and half the sheriff's deputies would be at the party. The rustlers had several hours of work ahead of them, herding the cattle through the fence and loading them into the truck. Daniel could bring a posse back with him in plenty of time.

Grinning, he turned his horse and set off at a jog. Willa would get what she wanted—he was playing by her rules. Hell, she could even come along and help them catch the bad guys. She was a better shot than most of the men, anyway.

Riding across the open range, Daniel didn't see the sixth man on the rustler's crew, the one they'd posted as lookout. And he didn't hear the crack of the rifle shot until after the bullet slammed into him from the left rear, knocking him clean out of the saddle.

BY 1:00 A.M., THE *POSADA* HAD wound down to a few good friends and family enjoying their fruit punch on the front terrace under a brilliant moon.

"Quite a party, Miss Willa." Nate lifted a cup in salute. "I never seen one like it in all my years on the Blue Moon."

Willa smiled as she watched him clink his glass with Lili's, who sat next to him on the wall. "I'm glad you enjoyed yourself."

"We all did." Next to her, Hobbs Sutton stretched his long arms wide. He let his hand come to rest on the back of her chair, just behind her shoulder. Not touching, quite. She supposed the dances they'd shared this evening encouraged him to hope for more—especially since Daniel had been so conspicuously absent from the party.

And she'd missed him every second. But why should tonight be different from every day of the past few weeks?

She shook her head slightly, trying to banish him from her thoughts yet again. Susannah and Toby had gone to bed more than an hour ago, worn out by the work and excitement of the day. Across the courtyard, Robbie sat by himself, staring at nothing she could see. She'd had no trouble with him since…well, since she'd broken off with Daniel. Of course. And the school reports were all positive. For three weeks he'd been a model student, the perfect son. Something would have to give soon, or he'd explode.

The thought made her smile. Hobbs leaned forward. "What are you thinking about?"

"It's nothing." She could have shared the joke with Daniel but not with a man she'd known all her life. "I suppose I could start gathering up these dishes—"

As she sat forward, she saw Robbie jerk his head up. In the next second, she caught the sound he'd heard first—the furious pounding of a horse's hooves galloping down the road. Willa turned and stood up in the same motion, looking northward… toward Daniel's place. The New Moon Ranch.

"It's Calypso!" Robbie vaulted the courtyard wall and ran toward the road, arms spread wide, standing directly in the horse's path. "Whoa, Cal. Whoa, there."

Eyes wide, nostrils flaring, the horse planted its front hooves and slid to a stop only inches from where Robbie stood. He grabbed the reins, which had been trailing on the ground. It was a miracle Cal hadn't tripped on them and hurt himself.

"It's okay," Robbie crooned to the animal as Willa came up. "You're all right." Calypso's chest was heaving with the effort of his breath. The foam on his legs indicated he'd galloped a fair distance at top speed.

"Did he escape the corral?" Willa voiced what she knew was a futile hope.

Hobbs looked at her from the other side of the horse. "I don't think so." He took the reins from Robbie and walked Cal in a circle so she could see his right side.

Daniel's boot was stuck in the right stirrup.

Willa gasped, and pressed her fist against her lips.

"I'm afraid Daniel was riding," the sheriff said. "And fell off. He's out there." He nodded north, toward Daniel's land and the Wild Horse Desert. "Somewhere."

"Well, what are we waiting for?" Nate stepped up. "Let's go find him!"

Chapter Fifteen

When Daniel came solidly back to consciousness, it was still dark. He must not have been out very long. Maybe Calypso would have stopped to graze somewhere nearby, and they could still get back to the barn…though he couldn't seem to remember what he'd planned to do when he got there.

The first step would be to get back on his feet. His head felt heavy, though, more than his neck muscles could manage. The effort of lifting his hand from the ground left him panting. He let his arm fall back to his side. Something was wrong. He shouldn't be this weak. What had happened?

He remembered riding but not why. He didn't remember falling. Opening his eyes, he tried to figure out his surroundings from what he could see. Rough, sandy dirt…not the grass pasture he recalled. When he turned his head, a black cloud formed in front of his eyes, and he had to wait for it to clear. Another sign of weakness. Blood loss? Why was he bleeding?

Above him, the starry night and bright moon he seemed to remember had been replaced with heavy cloud cover. Or…no. The sky wouldn't be so close. Hanging only a foot or so above him were leaves and branches. Some kind of tree. Or bush, to be so low to the ground. He appeared to be lying under a dense bush.

Okay, he'd fallen into some brush. He'd hit his head, which explained the threatened blackout, and even the bleeding. Head wounds could be messy. Still, he needed to crawl out into the open, locate his horse and get the hell home.

Pushing his palm against the earth, he grunted and groaned and forced his shoulders a few inches off the ground…until a shaft of pure agony shot through him. Daniel collapsed, which hurt every bit as much, and lay whimpering like a little kid until the pain faded enough to let him think.

Something wrong with the shoulder. In back, he decided, where he couldn't reach. Getting to the horse was going to be harder than he'd thought. Getting on the horse might be impossible.

So maybe he'd just rest awhile, gather his reserves. He'd feel better, be stronger in an hour or two…

A CONVOY OF TRUCKS RUMBLED UP the road toward the New Moon Ranch. Willa brought up the rear, having taken time to change out of her party clothes into jeans and boots. Robbie had waited for her, riding silently in the passenger seat.

When they reached Daniel's house, Hobbs Sutton was just coming out the front door. He walked over to her window. "No sign of trouble inside. Well, except for Trouble, asleep on the bed." She didn't smile at the joke.

The sheriff put a hand over hers on the steering wheel. "We'll find him, Willa. Everything's gonna be okay. He told me he'd call if he found the rustlers, and I haven't heard from dispatch all night."

"Maybe they found him first."

The sheriff shook his head. "Let's go on to the barn. Maybe he fell asleep in the office. Then we'll all look like fools…and be happy about it."

At the barn, though, there was no sign of Daniel in the office or anywhere else. While Nate and the men who'd come with them—hands from both ranches and a few deputies—fanned out over the surrounding ground, Willa stood gazing at Daniel's command center with Hobbs and Robbie.

"There was a break in the fence tonight." Hobbs pointed to a computer monitor, where a diagram of Daniel's perimeter fence showed up as a blue line. Beside Hobbs's finger, a red *X* flashed. "Here, on the northeast side."

"So he did go after the rustlers." Willa slapped her hand against the back of the desk chair. "You said he was going to call you."

"He told me he would. But he wasn't going to let them get away with it, either. If the choice was between catching the rustlers and letting them go…"

"Daniel would have gone in on his own." Willa shook her head. "I knew it would come to this."

Standing in the corner closest to the door, Robbie shifted his feet. "Maybe…maybe he didn't think it would be the rustlers."

Willa looked at him. "Why else would he go out there? He set this whole system up to catch rustlers."

"Well, maybe he'd been getting…some, um, false alarms."

Hobbs looked at Robbie. "You know something about that?"

Willa went to stand in front of her son. "Have you been talking to Daniel about this?"

"No." He kept his gaze on the floor. "But I—I came up here a few times, cut through his fence."

When Willa couldn't say anything, Hobbs took over. "Did you do this one?"

Robbie shook his head. "I stayed at the party all night."

"So the rustlers were out there. Daniel, thinking it might be another trick, went out to check." The sheriff turned on his heel and strode outside, calling for the men who'd come with them.

"We'll talk about this," Willa promised her son. "For now, sit down right there." She pointed at Daniel's chair. "And don't move until I get back."

ROBBIE DID AS HE WAS TOLD. He didn't…couldn't…fall asleep. He could picture what might have happened if Daniel ran into the rustlers. If Daniel was hurt, it would be his fault.

The red *X* flashed from the monitor until he thought he'd go crazy looking at it, so he turned the chair around to face the window. Beside the window was a photograph, hard to see in the dark. Disobeying his mom's instructions, Robbie crossed the room to get a better look.

He recognized the scene right away. His family—Toby, Susannah, Lili, Rosa, Mom and himself—in the courtyard on the afternoon after the Zapata rodeo. They'd gathered around the table for a minute, with Mom sitting and laughing up at something Toby said while Rosa and Lili set out food. Susannah was pouring drinks. Robbie saw himself at the edge of the picture with a frown on his face, looking directly at the camera.

Daniel must have taken the picture without them realizing— maybe he had one of those cell phones with a camera. He'd caught them all at that moment and then printed the picture out and put it on his wall. Even after Mom had told him not to see them anymore, the photograph was still there.

The man cared. And they all cared about him.

Maybe I do, too. Would you mind, Dad? Could I like him, at least a little?

No voice came out of the darkness, letting him know it would be okay. Robbie sat through the night, remembering his father, thinking about Daniel Trent, and wondering if he'd get the chance to make up for his mistakes.

DANIEL WOKE UP TO DAYLIGHT this time, but feeling worse.

"Better move," he mumbled to himself. "Not getting better just lying here."

He struggled for what seemed like hours just to roll from his side to his belly. Once he got his hands flat on the ground, underneath his shoulders, he let himself rest, recover his breath. He woke up sneezing sand and dirt out his nose.

"Okay. One pushup, that's all." He pushed, and fire blazed through his chest. Teeth gritted, Daniel ignored the pain. "Push... push...damn it, push..."

Finally, he got his left knee bent under him. Using hands, knee and his right toe, he crawled through the scrub he'd landed in. Branches and thorns scratched his face. He put his hand down on a patch of low-growing cactus and came away with spines in his palm, which burrowed deeper with every move.

He found a tree by banging his head into the trunk. Swearing as loudly as his dry throat would allow, Daniel gripped the tree with one hand, then the other, clawing his way over the rough bark until he could get his left foot flat on the ground. And then he wrapped his arms around the trunk to help drag his right leg in and straighten up.

Another black cloud passed across his vision, and he thought he would pass out again. The blessed tree kept him conscious as well as upright. After a time, he felt strong enough to lift his head and scan the horizon. He had a horse somewhere. Right? That's what he was looking for?

No horse. He made a slow, three-hundred-and-sixty degree survey of his surroundings. No animal that he could see.

For that matter, this didn't look like anywhere he remembered having been before. He couldn't recall a part of his ranch that resembled this dry, barren, wild place, and he thought he knew his land pretty well by now.

Where had he ended up on that ride he couldn't remember? How far had he come from familiar territory? Which direction was home?

He consulted the compass on his watch and decided to head west, because he'd reach the Mexican border eventually, and probably run into somebody who could help him. Assuming he survived. Some water would probably make that more of a certainty. Maybe he'd stumble into a creek along the way.

But he stumbled only a few steps beyond his savior tree, over a rock that hadn't been there seconds before. The sun on his back was warm, the ground under his cheek surprisingly comfortable. Daniel decided he needed more rest before trying again. He'd just lie here and think about Willa for a while. Then he'd be ready to start over....

"THEY'RE HERE," TOBY CALLED, after dark on Sunday night. He'd been watching the front of the house all day. "Nate and Mom are here!"

Rosa gathered with the rest of the family in the entry hall, gazing hopefully as Nate and Willa came through the front door.

"Nothin'," Nate told them. "We didn't find him anywhere on the ranch." At a gesture from Willa, he followed her down the hallway toward the kitchen.

"Did you look outside the fence?" Rosa went after them, with Lili and the children behind her. "Could he have gone into the desert and...and been left there?"

Willa sank into a chair at the kitchen table and buried her head in her arms.

"We rode the perimeter," Nate said. Lili put a plate down in front of him. "We saw where the cattle had been driven through the fence and onto the truck, with the tracks of ATVs. We searched for a mile outward in all directions. We couldn't find him."

"Do you suppose they took him with them?" Rosa asked.

"Maybe." Nate swallowed down several bites, then looked over at Willa. "Miss Willa, you need to sit up and eat. We got more to do and you're gonna need your strength."

She didn't say anything, didn't move. After a few minutes, though, she made a sound...a sob. As they all stared, frozen with shock, Willa's shoulders began to shake. Her hands clenched. Without apology or inhibition, she sat there in the kitchen and cried all the tears she'd dammed up for two years, plus all the new tears from recent days.

Rosa nodded to herself. It was about time.

The storm abated eventually, when the old sorrows, at least, were spent. Toby and Susannah went to stand behind their mother, patting her shoulder, stroking her hair. Rosa sat down in the next chair and took one of her niece's fists between her hands, stroking and murmuring until the fingers relaxed. Lili made a pot of tea and set a cup within reach.

When she was ready, Willa sat up, wiped her eyes with her free hand and reached for the tea.

"I'm sorry," she said in a husky voice. "I didn't mean to inflict that on anybody." She gave her aunts a tiny smile, a larger one to Toby and Susannah. "We'll find him. I know we will. He's a strong man and he'll be waiting for us to get there." She took a deep breath and looked around the kitchen, as if waking from a long sleep. Her eyes widened. "Where's Roberto?"

Like children playing a game, they all imitated her, looking around the kitchen as if Robbie had simply hidden himself for a joke. "He was here when you came home," Susannah said. "I didn't see him leave."

"I'll check his room." Toby left the kitchen at a run, and came back quickly. "He's not there. I don't think he's in the house."

"Maybe he went to the barn to be alone." Lili refilled Willa's cup. "He's spent some time out there today."

Willa nodded. "That's probably it. He bears some responsibility for what's happened. He's got a lot to think about."

But when she called the barn, where some of their hands were resting up after the day of searching, the news wasn't good.

"He's not in the barn." Willa hung up the phone but didn't face them right away. "And Tar is missing." Turning around at last, she showed her worried frown to Rosa, Lili and Nate. "He's taken his horse and gone out by himself at night to look for Daniel."

ROBBIE HAD SPENT A LOT OF TIME—more than his mother ever knew about—in the desert outside the boundaries of the Blue Moon Ranch. He'd camped there with his dad, learning to identify the plants and trees and animals that thrived on the hot, dry plains of south Texas. His dad had taught him tracking skills, too, and ways to avoid being tracked. On winter days, when he could escape school and work—and Toby—he and Tar would pretend they were explorers, scouting new territory on a distant planet.

If anybody could find Daniel Trent in the Wild Horse Desert, it would be him.

He started at the break in the fence the rustlers had made and moved in expanding circles from there. He saw all the tracks Nate had mentioned. The cattle truck and the ATVs veered to the left, eventually, in the direction of the road west to Mexico.

But there were other tracks, Robbie thought, tracks that had been erased by someone who didn't want to be followed. He started his circles again from that point, noticing how smooth the sandy ground appeared, as if swept by a broom or a large brush. Or maybe by someone with a tree branch, obscuring his tracks.

The moon passed overhead as he worked, checking out clumps of bushes and groups of trees, making sure the shadows of boulders hid only rocks and dirt. He didn't get tired, and he didn't stop. This was his problem, and he would make it right.

He didn't know what time it was when he heard the first groan. Tar halted and they both stayed still, listening to the desert sounds. A breeze ruffled stalks of grass and the leaves of trees. Here and there, a lizard scrabbled across a rock, or some sand. An owl hooted in the distance.

Not too far away, someone moaned.

Robbie stood up in his stirrups, peering into the night. "Daniel? It's Rob. Make some more noise. Throw a rock. Help me find you."

He'd almost given up when a noise came to him, a strange, whining, singing sound. Robbie choked back a laugh when he realized it was singing.

"Over hill…dale…hit the…trail…as the caissons…go rolling… Oh, it's hi-hi hee…field artillery…" The U.S. Army's theme song. He remembered his dad singing it.

Walking Tar slowly, carefully, Robbie followed the sound. In the distance, he saw an old mesquite tree twisted by the wind, with a sharp-edged shadow underneath it—a shadow slanted in a different direction than every other shadow on the ground.

"Yes!" He urged Tar to a jog and reached the mesquite in a matter of minutes. Throwing himself out of the saddle, he dropped to his knees beside the man on the ground. "I've got you, Daniel. You're gonna be okay."

"Good to know." The man tried to roll over to look at him but clearly didn't have the strength.

Robbie used both hands to ease him backward and caught a sharp breath. "You've been shot!"

Daniel nodded. "That would explain the way I feel." He shivered, his teeth chattering. "Cold," he said weakly. "Need to sleep."

"Don't sleep. You have to help me get you back to the house." On his feet again, Robbie tied Tar's reins to a branch of the tree. "Come on, Daniel." He leaned over and hooked his hands under the injured man's armpits. "You gotta get up."

"N-n-not th-that way." Trent opened his eyes halfway. "Roll me over to the f-f-front."

"Are you sure?"

"D-don't argue."

Robbie did as he was told, and rolled Daniel face-down in the dirt. Then he added his strength to the effort it took to get the man's knee bent beneath him and his shoulders off the ground.

"Good," Daniel panted. "Now I get up."

He was heavier than he looked, and Robbie bore almost all of his weight before Daniel finally stood upright. With the injured man's arm over his shoulders, they walked the ten feet to Tar's left side.

Daniel looked up at the saddle. "C-c-can't d-do it. L-leave me here, b-bring b-b-back help." He started to sag in the middle.

"No!" Robbie held him up. "I'm taking you with me. You're getting in that saddle."

The major looked down at him sideways. "Yeah?"

Robbie set his jaw. "Yeah."

Afterward, he could never say just how they did it. But somehow, Daniel ended up astride the horse, tied there with the rope Robbie always carried on the saddle.

Then he and Tar walked Major Trent out of the Wild Horse Desert.

"WILL YOU LOOK THERE?" Standing at the fence line of the New Moon Ranch, Nate gestured out into the desert.

Willa followed the direction of the foreman's pointing finger. In the predawn darkness, she couldn't see anything. "I don't…"

Then she distinguished movement, like one shadow separating from another. A white oval became a face. Robbie's face.

"It's them!" She tightened her legs, and Monty jumped forward into a lope, lengthening quickly to a gallop. Cheers and hoofbeats followed her, and truck engines roared, but they couldn't catch up. Willa beat them all by a quarter of a mile.

Once they were seen, Robbie and Tar stayed where they were. Monty made a sliding stop just ten feet away. Leaving the horse's reins on his neck, Willa hit the ground running.

And then she was hugging Robbie, rubbing his head, scolding

and kissing and crying all at the same time. "You should never take off like that by yourself. Never, do you hear me?"

He grinned and gave her a one-armed hug in return. "I hear you."

Letting him go, she turned to touch the man on the horse. "Daniel? Daniel, are you awake?"

He didn't stir, and she looked over at Robbie. "Are you sure he's…"

At that moment, Nate arrived on horseback. Lili and Rosa had brought the truck, with Toby and Susannah. Hobbs and two deputies pulled up in a sheriff's department van. An ambulance had just reached the top of the last ridge and was starting down the hill.

The men took over, lifting Daniel off the horse and laying him back on the ground. Willa stood with her arms wrapped around her waist, her lips pressed between her teeth as Rosa handed Nate a jug of water and a cloth. The older man sponged off the scratched and bloodied face. "Hey, Boss, wake up. We got you back now. Need to ask some questions."

No one breathed. Daniel didn't move. Susannah pressed against Willa's side. "Is he going to be okay, Mom?"

"Sure, he is." Did she believe it herself? "He'll wake up in a minute."

The ambulance arrived, and a new set of attendants pushed Nate and Hobbs out of the way. "Gunshot to the left shoulder," she heard someone comment. "Massive blood loss."

"Severe concussion," one of the other EMTs responded. "Temp one-oh-three. Probably infected."

If Daniel would only open his eyes…if he could say just a word before they took him away…

But in minutes he'd been lifted into the back of the ambulance. Before she could ask to ride along, the doors were shut. And then Daniel disappeared once again.

"Come with me." Hobbs put an arm around her shoulders. "We'll get you to the hospital."

She glanced at her children, her aunts and Nate. "I'll call," she promised.

And then she buckled herself into the sheriff's van for the endless drive into Laredo.

"YOU, AGAIN?"

Daniel opened his eyes to a blur of gray and white. Gradually, his eyes focused on a white doctor's coat over a pair of faded surgical scrubs. "I guess so."

Cool fingers touched his cheek and turned his face away from the pillow. "Remember me? Dr. Dobbins. I saw you last time you showed up in the ER."

"I remember." He wasn't sure what kept him on the bed. His body felt light enough to float away.

"You lost more blood than we usually allow," the doctor said from somewhere beyond his range of vision. "And we don't recommend spending thirty-six hours in the desert without food or water."

"I'm better at giving orders than following them."

"Like most men. Fortunately, I'm a very good doctor and you're going to be okay. The bullet nicked a vein and plowed through some muscle, which will take a while to heal. We'll keep you a few days, make sure that pesky infection you kept yourself amused with is knocked back with some IV antibiotics, and then we'll send you home, where you will stay off horses and out of the desert for at least a month. Got that?"

"Got it." The way he felt right now, he wouldn't have the energy for horses or anything else for at least a year.

The next time he woke, the room light had been dimmed and only blackness showed behind the window blinds. He'd spent many nights awake on a hospital bed, pondering his past, wondering if his future included a home on the range.

After the latest fiasco, he didn't have to wonder anymore. He'd surely topped any limit there might be to the number of mistakes allowed a beginning rancher. He'd had great advice, good help, and the best of intentions. Yet he'd ended up with dead cattle. Despite his high-tech methods, he'd botched his chance to catch the rustlers—they'd probably made off with most of his herd that night. And how ludicrous was it that he, an Army officer and decorated war veteran, had let himself be ambushed by an amateur sniper and hauled into the desert to die?

He'd set out to prove himself as a man and a rancher. What he'd proved was that he should find a nice, safe desk job somewhere. Take up computer programming, or systems analysis, efficiency management…he'd swallowed a bellyful of training in the military. A bum leg and an overdeveloped hero complex wouldn't be such a handicap in a padded office cubicle under fluorescent lights.

Just don't let him loose under the wide Texas skies. Willa had been right from the beginning. He didn't belong.

Nate showed up the next morning. "You're looking a sight better than the last time I saw you." He straddled a chair backwards, resting his arms across the seatback. "We'll have you back on the job in no time." He squinted through one eye. "Well, maybe you oughta wait till after Christmas, anyway."

"I don't think so."

Nate cocked an eyebrow in question.

"I'm cashing in, so to speak." The foreman didn't move, forcing Daniel to explain. "I'm going to give the land back to Willa. This ranching life…I don't think it's what I want, after all."

"Yeah, right. Tell me another one, why don't you?"

"I'm not kidding. I've been thinking about it for the past

month or so. I've got some other job options lined up already. I want to stay for the full term of my agreement with…with Willa. But I'll be gone before Christmas."

Chapter Sixteen

Nate told Lili, and Lili told Rosa. "He's leaving the New Moon."

"No, he's not." They were wrapping presents for Willa and the children in their bedroom Thursday night. "Willa will convince him to stay."

"What makes you think so? She hasn't said a word about him since that night at the hospital. Once she knew he would recover, she came home and hasn't seen him since."

"Do you doubt that she loves him?"

"No."

"Well, then, she'll change her mind. She'll persuade him to marry her and live here on the ranch."

Lili shook her head. "You're awfully optimistic."

"I'm right. You'll see. Just as I was right about you and Nate." Watching her sister, she saw the blush begin and bloom brightly in Lili's cheeks. "Wasn't I?"

"Y-yes."

"Has he asked you to marry him?"

"Not in so many words."

Rosa clucked her tongue. "What did he say?"

Lili gave a mischievous smile. "He said, 'Lili, dear, I would die a happy man if I could enjoy your cooking every day for the rest of my life.'"

Rosa laughed. "You're right—not in so many words. I suspect you'll get the precise words by Christmas."

"Oh, I hope so," Lili said. "I do hope so."

GETTING TO LAREDO WASN'T EASY for a kid of thirteen, especially when you couldn't ask your mom to drive you, and when you had school from eight until three every day of the week and chores all afternoon.

In his desperation, Robbie finally took the principal into his confidence on Friday. After listening to his explanation, Mrs. Abrams agreed he had a responsibility to complete, and she consented to help him out. She checked him out of school at lunchtime on Friday, drove him all the way to the hospital in Laredo and said she would wait thirty minutes while he talked with Daniel Trent.

To his surprise, Daniel was seated in a chair in his room, instead of lying in the bed. Under his robe, he had on one of those stupid gowns they made you wear. His legs were bare above gray slippers. And he had tubes running into his arm from bags hanging on a metal stand.

His grin was the same, though. "Well, hello. You're a long way from home."

"I got a ride from school. I only have thirty minutes."

"That's time for a good visit. Have a seat." He motioned to the chair beside him. "I'm glad you're here. I haven't had a chance to say thanks for coming to find me."

Robbie felt himself blush. "I made you go out there. I had to bring you back."

"The rustlers were the reason I was out there."

Here was the hardest part. "But you didn't get help because you thought it was a false alarm. That's because I tricked you. I cut the wire, four times. And ran away."

"I see." Daniel was looking at him, not in anger or even disappointment. He just seemed…interested. "Did you plan for me to get caught by the rustlers?"

"I—I don't think so. I mean, I never sat down and thought it out." He felt stupid for ever coming up with such a dumb trick to begin with. "I just wanted to make you mad."

"What did you think would happen if I got mad?"

"I thought you'd leave," Robbie said in a low voice. "I wanted you to leave."

Daniel nodded. "Well, you've got your wish. I'll be leaving Sunday, probably. Monday, at the latest."

"But you can't." Robbie leaned forward in his chair. "Most of the bad stuff that happened was because of me. I was a baby, a brat. I thought you'd ruin everything."

"You've had a hard time, Rob. Losing your dad like that was tough. I don't blame you for wanting to keep your life the way it was with him."

"But things change, whether you want them to or not."

Daniel chuckled. "You're pretty smart. Some people never learn that particular truth."

"And I know now that you'd be good to us. To Mom. And you wouldn't try to push my dad out of the way or make us forget. I don't hate you." He looked down at his hands for a second. "I don't hate my dad, either."

"I know that. And I appreciate your trust. But—"

"So you really do have to stay." He reached out to clasp Daniel's hand with his own. "Mom was happy when she could be with you. Toby and Susannah…Lili and Rosa…they like you. We could be a—a family."

As he watched, Daniel swallowed hard. "That's a tempting invitation, Rob. I care about all of you. I really do." He sighed. "But I don't think I've got what it takes to keep trying, day after day, month after month. Ranch work requires more strength, more energy, than I have to give. I hate failing, but I can't stay and do more damage than I already have."

Robbie couldn't give up. "Look, if it's Mom, you just have to give her some time. She'll come around."

"That's between your mom and me." Daniel got slowly to his feet, drawing his hand away from Robbie's. "Thanks for your confidence, Rob, and your friendship. It means a lot that you changed your mind." He glanced at the clock. "Your thirty minutes is about gone. You'd better say goodbye."

Hesitating, staring at his hands, Robbie tried to think of something to say, something to persuade Daniel to give them another chance.

Someone knocked at the door. "Is Robbie Mercado there?" Mrs. Abrams asked.

"I'm here." Feeling tired and sad, he got to his feet.

"We need to leave, Robbie."

"Yes, ma'am." He glanced at Daniel one last time. "She loves you, you know. I knew it from the first time she said your name. I guess that's why I was so afraid. 'Bye."

He held up his chin as he left. But he was grateful for the comfort of Mrs. Abrams's hand on his shoulder as they walked down the hall.

WILLA HADN'T ATTENDED church often since Jamie had left for Iraq and especially not since he'd been killed. The children went with Rosa and Lili, but she usually worked Sunday morning, in the barn, on the bills…there was no shortage of tasks needing her attention.

Like so many others, however, she wouldn't miss church at Christmas. There would be a mass on Christmas Eve, of course, but she got dressed on Sunday morning, as well, and left with the aunts and the children.

The church in Zapata was beautifully decorated for the holy

day, with its own elaborate *nacimiento* behind the altar. Candles flickered in the draft created by the presence of so many people, while the rich tang of incense hung in the air. Sitting in the pew that Rosa and Lili considered their own, participating in the familiar patterns of the service, Willa absorbed the sights and sounds around her, searching for comfort. Searching for answers.

Daniel had decided to leave. All she had to do was stay home this afternoon, and the Mercado land would remain intact. No New Moon Ranch, no stranger's cattle grazing the family's range. Nate had told her Daniel would leave her the cattle to keep or sell as she wished, and Calypso, as well. He would, however, be taking Trouble with him.

She hadn't visited him in the hospital, because she didn't know what to say. He'd been coming to get backup when he was shot—that meant he was trying to meet the demands she'd made. If he'd gone after the rustlers alone, he might not have been injured. Or he might have been dead. There was, Hobbs said, no way to tell.

Which pretty much summed up life in general, didn't it? You couldn't tell about the outcome of a decision until after you'd made it. She'd married Jamie because she believed they would have a good life, growing old together on the Blue Moon. Look how that had turned out.

Then she'd determined to go on alone, to tend the ranch and her children and never, ever care enough to hurt that much again. And she'd succeeded, more or less, until Daniel Trent had walked…limped…into her life and swept her off her feet. No matter how often and how strongly she'd tried to deny him, and herself, she'd been in love with him from the beginning. Her fury over his plan concerning the rustlers had been in direct proportion to her need and desire and worry for him.

"Mom!" Beside her, Toby gave a jerk of his head. They were supposed to be kneeling at this point in the service.

Willa eased forward onto the kneeling bench he'd set down, braced her arms on the pew in front of her and bowed her head. She hadn't prayed since Jamie's death. She wasn't sure she was praying now. But she tried to open her mind, allowing whatever guidance, blessing or wisdom was available to flow into her.

Could she take the risk of loving Daniel? Could she risk letting him go?

At the end of the Mass, the youngest children performed *la pastorella*—a re-enactment of the birth of Jesus, the visit of the shepherds to the stable and the journey of the three kings.

Toby leaned over to whisper, "Was I that cute when I played José?"

Willa winked at him. "Much cuter."

He sat back with a satisfied nod. "I thought so."

After the service, as they all settled into the car and buckled their seatbelts, Toby piped up again. "Can we eat lunch in town today? Please?"

"I have stew simmering," Rosa told him. "Lili had planned to make cornbread."

"But—"

Willa turned to Rosa, in the front passenger seat. "Would you mind if we saved the stew for dinner? I would like to do some shopping before we go back home."

Her aunt gazed at her for a moment. "If that's what you need to do, Willa. Of course the stew will wait for dinner." She smiled. "And there's plenty of it."

EVEN WITH NATE'S HELP, the process of packing up Daniel's few belongings seemed to go slowly. He could blame it on the dog—every time he put clothes in a suitcase, Trouble dragged them out again and ran through the house, trailing clean shirts, socks and underwear after him. The washing machine chose that morning to spew sand into the tub with the water, so he couldn't wash the towels and sheets Lili and Rosa had provided until after Nate figured out and fixed the problem.

Then, for the first time ever, Trouble decided to investigate the container of food left to thaw on the kitchen counter for lunch. In the process, dog, cabinets, walls and floor took on a thick, tasty coat of tomato sauce.

As Daniel wiped off the last of the red splotches on the counter, he heard the slam of several car doors, and then the high, excited voices of children.

The Mercado kids and aunts, he guessed. Coming to say goodbye. He stood for a second with his eyes squeezed shut, his hands gripping the sill of the sink.

I can do this. I have to.

By the time he reached the front door, he had his grin in place. "Hey, guys," he started. Then stopped, speechless.

Willa stood alone on his front stoop, holding a big cardboard box. Behind her, Toby and Susannah knelt on the ground, taking strings of lights out of packages. Robbie stood in the truck bed, uncoiling an outdoor extension cord. Beside him in the bed lay an evergreen tree, its branches tightly bound in bright orange netting.

Daniel looked back at Willa. "What's going on?"

"We thought you would want an Anglo Christmas—the tree, the wreath and lights, all that stuff. But…" She pushed past him into the house. "But we thought we could educate you on our traditions, too. So I brought a small *nacimiento*—nativity scene. The tree can go in front of the window. And we'll put the nativity—" She walked to the empty bookshelf near his chair "—here."

"Willa." He had to try twice to get his voice to work. "I'm leaving. You know that. I don't need…want…Christmas here."

Crouched over the box, she didn't seem to have heard him. "Jamie's parents bought this set on a trip to Mexico, and we used to put it in the boys' room when they were younger." She held up a figure. "The animals are especially fun. See the expression on the donkey's face?"

"See the expression on my face?" He reached down, grasped her arm and lifted her to her feet. "What are you trying to say?"

She turned slightly away to place the donkey on the bookshelf, then took a deep breath and faced him again. "Don't go, Daniel. Please stay here with us. With me."

He shook his head. "You win, Willa. I'm not good enough. Not cut out for ranching. Juan Angelo came to the hospital on Friday and I signed the papers. You get your land back."

Her hands went to her hips. "So you're just going to quit? If you can walk away, then maybe you really don't have what it takes."

"You got it."

She eyed him for a minute. "Or maybe you lied to me when you told me you loved me."

"No." He went to stand by the window, watching the kids string lights around the posts of the carport. "I never lied to you."

"Then how can you leave? When I love you, too?"

Daniel swallowed hard. "You never said that."

"I was still working it out. And you made me mad." She joined him at the window and put a hand on his arm. "I was terrified when I knew you were missing. I might have lost you, and I thought that would be the worst thing that could happen."

"You've been through it once, already."

"Yes, I have. But guess what I realized?"

"I don't know."

"There's something even worse than losing the person you love."

"What's that?"

"Never having loved them at all."

He looked at her and saw the light in her eyes, the smile on her face. "You think?"

Willa nodded. "I know. I loved Jamie, and we had a good life. He left me three children I adore and a ranch I'm proud of. If I had been afraid to marry him because he might die or leave, I would have missed all of that."

Stepping even closer, she placed her hands on his chest. "And if I lose you because I'm afraid of what might happen, or because I let you doubt yourself, then I'll miss all of the joy we could find together. I don't want to miss that joy, Daniel. Please, stay. Stay and marry me."

A knock on the window drew their attention outside. Toby, Susannah and Rob stood on the other side of the glass, all of them wide-eyed with an easily understood question.

"Yes," Daniel told them. "Now go away." He pulled the blinds closed for good measure. Then he bent his head to Willa's for a kiss.

She put her fingers against his lips. "Tell me," she ordered. "I want to hear it."

"Yes," Daniel said. "Yes, I'll marry you. I may not be the world's greatest cowboy, but I'll love you every day of my life." He kissed her, then lifted his head and grinned. "Which, by the way, lady, is a no-risk guarantee!"

THE MERCADO *NAVIDAD* CELEBRATION was in full swing. They'd attended midnight Mass—the Rooster Mass, it was called, for the bird that had announced the dawn on the day of Jesú's birth. Now they were all seated around the dining room table, enjoying the feast Lili and Rosa had prepared.

Sipping on fruit punch, Willa leaned back in her chair and watched the celebration with pleasure. Nate and Lili sat together on the other side of the table, caught up in the private world of a newly engaged couple. The diamond on Lili's finger wasn't large, but the stars in her eyes would have outshone a much fancier stone.

Willa knew the feeling. Daniel's hand cradled hers on the arm of her chair. She turned her head to look at him and found his gaze waiting.

"Having fun?" He leaned close so she could hear him despite the noise…or maybe just so he could kiss her cheek.

"It's wonderful. I've never seen everybody so happy."

"And we haven't even opened presents yet."

She squeezed his fingers. "I've got mine right here."

"Me, too." He raised their joined hands and kissed her fingers. "But I think Toby wants something more tangible."

The child in question left his seat and came to stand behind them, with a hand on each of their shoulders. "Is it time, yet?"

Willa pretended to think. "For bed? Well, it is after two."

He scowled at her. "For presents, Mom. When do we get to open our presents?"

Willa glanced at Rosa, who nodded. Then she looked back at her son. "I guess now is as good a time as any."

Toby whooped, and shouted to his brother and sister to join him in the parlor. The adults followed more slowly but arrived in time to see the flurry of wrapping paper and the cries of pleasure as gifts were revealed.

Willa stood with Daniel behind her, his arms wrapped around her, his heart beating strongly against her back. "Three months ago," she said, more to herself than to him, "I would never have believed life could be this good again."

"We're very lucky." He rubbed his cheek against her hair. "We've both been given a second chance at life…and love."

Willa nodded. "You're right. It is good luck." She thought for a moment. "And you know what they say. Luck like this…"

Looking up at him over her shoulder, she waited for Daniel to finish her thought.

He gave her that wonderful grin. "Only comes around once in a blue moon?"

Willa smiled, nestling more closely into his embrace. "Exactly."

* * * * *

SPECIAL EDITION®

LIFE, LOVE AND FAMILY

These contemporary romances will strike a chord with you as heroines juggle life and relationships on their way to true love.

New York Times *bestselling author Linda Lael Miller brings you a BRAND-NEW contemporary story featuring her fan-favorite McKettrick family.*

Meg McKettrick is surprised to be reunited with her high school flame, Brad O'Ballivan. After enjoying a career as a country-and-western singer, Brad aches for a home and family…and seeing Meg again makes him realize he still loves her. But their pride manages to interfere with love…until an unexpected matchmaker gets involved.

Turn the page for a sneak preview of
THE McKETTRICK WAY
by Linda Lael Miller
On sale November 20,
wherever books are sold.

Brad shoved the truck into gear and drove to the bottom of the hill, where the road forked. Turn left, and he'd be home in five minutes. Turn right, and he was headed for Indian Rock.

He had no damn business going to Indian Rock.

He had nothing to say to Meg McKettrick, and if he never set eyes on the woman again, it would be two weeks too soon.

He turned right.

He couldn't have said why.

He just drove straight to the Dixie Dog Drive-In.

Back in the day, he and Meg used to meet at the Dixie Dog, by tacit agreement, when either of them had been away. It had been some kind of universe thing, purely intuitive.

Passing familiar landmarks, Brad told himself he ought to turn around. The old days were gone. Things had ended badly between him and Meg anyhow, and she wasn't going to be at the Dixie Dog.

He kept driving.

He rounded a bend, and there was the Dixie Dog. Its big neon sign, a giant hot dog, was all lit up and going through its corny sequence—first it was covered in red squiggles of light, meant to suggest ketchup, and then yellow, for mustard.

Brad pulled into one of the slots next to a speaker, rolled down the truck window and ordered.

A girl roller-skated out with the order about five minutes later.

When she wheeled up to the driver's window, smiling, her eyes went wide with recognition, and she dropped the tray with a clatter.

Silently Brad swore. Damn if he hadn't forgotten he was a famous country singer.

The girl, a skinny thing wearing too much eye makeup, immediately started to cry. "I'm sorry!" she sobbed, squatting to gather up the mess.

"It's okay," Brad answered quietly, leaning to look down at her, catching a glimpse of her plastic name tag. "It's okay, Mandy. No harm done."

"I'll get you another dog and a shake right away, Mr. O'Ballivan!"

"Mandy?"

She stared up at him pitifully, sniffling. Thanks to the copious tears, most of the goop on her eyes had slid south. "Yes?"

"When you go back inside, could you not mention seeing me?"

"But you're Brad O'Ballivan!"

"Yeah," he answered, suppressing a sigh. "I know."

She rolled a little closer. "You wouldn't happen to have a picture you could autograph for me, would you?"

"Not with me," Brad answered.

"You could sign this napkin, though," Mandy said. "It's only got a little chocolate on the corner."

Brad took the paper napkin and her order pen, and scrawled his name. Handed both items back through the window.

She turned and whizzed back toward the side entrance to the Dixie Dog.

Brad waited, marveling that he hadn't considered incidents like this one before he'd decided to come back home. In retrospect, it seemed shortsighted, to say the least, but the truth was, he'd expected to be—Brad O'Ballivan.

Presently Mandy skated back out again, and this time she managed to hold on to the tray.

"I didn't tell a soul!" she whispered. "But Heather and Darlene *both* asked me why my mascara was all smeared." Efficiently she hooked the tray onto the bottom edge of the window.

Brad extended payment, but Mandy shook her head.

"The boss said it's on the house, since I dumped your first order on the ground."

He smiled. "Okay, then. Thanks."

Mandy retreated, and Brad was just reaching for the food when a bright red Blazer whipped into the space beside his. The driver's door sprang open, crashing into the metal speaker, and somebody got out in a hurry.

Something quickened inside Brad.

And in the next moment Meg McKettrick was standing practically on his running board, her blue eyes blazing.

Brad grinned. "I guess you're not over me after all," he said.

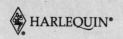

HARLEQUIN®

American ★ *Romance*®

Kate Merrill had grown up convinced
that the most attractive men were incapable
of ever settling down. Yet the harder she
resisted the superstar photographer
Tyler Nichols, the more persistent the
handsome world traveler became.
So by the time Christmas arrived, there
was only one wish on her holiday list—
that she was wrong!

LOOK FOR

THE CHRISTMAS DATE

BY

Michele Dunaway

**Available December
wherever you buy books**

REQUEST YOUR FREE BOOKS!
2 FREE NOVELS PLUS 2
FREE GIFTS!

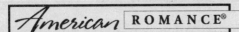

Heart, Home & Happiness!

HAR07

Get ready to meet

THREE WISE WOMEN

with stories by

DONNA BIRDSELL,
LISA CHILDS

and

SUSAN CROSBY.

Don't miss these three unforgettable stories about modern-day women and the love and new lives they find on Christmas.

Look for *Three Wise Women*
Available December wherever you buy books.

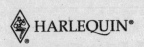

HARLEQUIN®

American **ROMANCE**®

COMING NEXT MONTH

#1189 THE RANCHER'S CHRISTMAS BABY by Cathy Gillen Thacker
Texas Legacies: The Carrigans
As teenagers, best friends Amy Carrigan and Teddy McCabe promised each other that if they didn't find their soul mates by thirty, they'd start their own family. Now, with Amy's biological clock ticking overtime, the sexy rancher decides to pop the question. But marriage brings more than they bargained for. Will love bloom in time to ring in the New Year with a Carrigan/McCabe baby?

#1190 TEXAN FOR THE HOLIDAYS by Victoria Chancellor
Brody's Crossing
No sooner has Scarlett shouted, "California, here I come!" than her clunker of a car breaks down. But there are worse places to be stranded than Brody's Crossing, especially when local lawyer James Brody is dying to show her how they celebrate the holidays in their quaint Texas town. Scarlett promised herself she'd be in Los Angeles by the New Year…but she's feeling more Texan by the minute!

#1191 THE CHRISTMAS DATE by Michele Dunaway
Kate Merrill had grown up convinced that the most attractive men were incapable of ever settling down. Yet the harder she resisted superstar photographer Tyler Nichols, the more persistent the handsome world traveler became. So by the time Christmas arrived, there was only one wish on her holiday list—that she was wrong!

#1192 WITH THIS RING by Lee McKenzie
A Convenient Proposal
Brent Borden had always imagined that Leslie Durrance was happy on her pedestal. Until she ran—in a thunderstorm, dripping diamonds, wedding dress and all—into the construction worker's arms. This was Brent's chance to show the poor little rich girl that maybe Mr. *Right* could come from the *wrong* side of town.

www.eHarlequin.com

HARCNM1107